# THE
# CRYSTAL
# CAT

*Also by Velda Johnston*

SHADOW BEHIND THE CURTAIN

VOICE IN THE NIGHT

THE OTHER KAREN

THE FATEFUL SUMMER

THE STONE MAIDEN

A PRESENCE IN THE EMPTY ROOM

THE PEOPLE FROM THE SEA

THE SILVER DOLPHIN

THE HOUR BEFORE MIDNIGHT

THE ETRUSCAN SMILE

DEVERON HALL

THE FRENCHMAN

A ROOM WITH DARK MIRRORS

THE HOUSE ON THE LEFT BANK

I CAME TO THE HIGHLANDS

THE WHITE PAVILION

MASQUERADE IN VENICE

THE LATE MRS. FONSELL

THE MOURNING TREES

THE FACE IN THE SHADOWS

THE PEOPLE ON THE HILL

THE LIGHT IN THE SWAMP

THE PHANTOM COTTAGE

I CAME TO A CASTLE

A HOWLING IN THE WOODS

HOUSE ABOVE HOLLYWOOD

ALONG A DARK PATH

# THE CRYSTAL CAT

### Velda Johnston

DODD, MEAD & COMPANY

NEW YORK

Published by Dodd, Mead & Company, Inc.
79 Madison Avenue, New York, N.Y. 10016
Distributed in Canada by
McClelland and Stewart Limited, Toronto
Manufactured in the United States of America
Designed by Helen Winfield
FIRST EDITION

*Library of Congress Cataloging in Publication Data*

Johnston, Velda.
The crystal cat.

I. Title.
PS3560.O394C7   1985   813'.54   85-6999
ISBN 0-396-08731-0

*For Dennis Starin,
and also for Mary Starin*

8

# ONE

I HAD NEVER dreamed that I would return to Wessex, that Connecticut town where I had spent the first six years of my life. All through the rest of my childhood and my growing-up years, the very thought of the place filled me with unease. And yet eventually I did find myself back there in that pretty village, where exurbanites in casually expensive clothes moved along the sidewalks past the fine old houses, and where, at least for me, the sparkling country air held a nameless menace.

Why did I go back there? I met a man. And I did not meet him in Manhattan, where I would have shunned him as soon as I learned the name of his hometown. I met him in Venice, that most seductive of cities, where if you're young and single, and most especially if you're somewhat on the rebound, you're apt to do something unwise.

That particular day in Venice, a sweltering one in August, I had spent several hours wandering in and out of ancient churches. Perhaps it was the alternation between near darkness and dazzling light that gave me a headache. The churches, where a few elderly women knelt in prayer, and whispering tourists waited, usually in vain, for a sacristan to turn on the lights above some famous

1

Titian or Veronese canvas, were filled with gloom. By contrast, the world outside—cobblestoned squares where cats dozed on the copings of old wells, and green-brown canals spanned by humpbacked bridges—was bathed by light so intense that it seemed to stab upward from paving stones and sun-dazzled water into my eyes. Head throbbing, I returned to my hotel room, closed the window shutters, and lay down in my slip on the bed, an impressive piece of furniture, which combined a fake antique headboard, all dark red velvet and gilt cupids, with the most modern of innerspring mattresses. Almost instantly I was asleep.

Sometime later I came awake to see dim light filtering through the shutters. Late afternoon light? Probably. I had a sense that I had napped for at least an hour. As I lay there, still half asleep, and grateful that my headache was gone, I heard my Aunt Ellen say, "Well, I do think it's bad luck that you had to run into him here, when we've got Linda with us."

Her voice came from the little balcony outside the room next to mine. Unaware that I had returned from my solitary sightseeing, she was discussing me with someone, almost certainly my Uncle Brad. I pictured them sitting out there in black wrought-iron chairs, a couple who looked almost comically alike—both brunette, both shorter than average and a few pounds overweight, both with slightly retroussé noses that made them look younger than their fifty-odd years.

I mustn't lie here, eavesdropping on the two dear people who had raised me. I sat up, swung my feet out of bed, and reached for my lightweight navy robe draped over a chair back.

Uncle Brad asked, "Why are you so upset? Just because he lives in Wessex?"

"Isn't that reason enough?"

With the robe in my hand, I sat motionless on the edge of the bed.

Wessex, where my mother had died by drowning. I had not witnessed her death, of course. And yet, perhaps because of adult conversation I had overheard, I had grown up with the mental image of her lying face down in that woodland pool, outspread long blond hair and thin white nightgown stirred by the current.

"We've been having such a good time," Aunt Ellen said. "I think it's been just what Linda needed after that awful experience."

I knew what she meant. The previous summer I had made the not uncommon error of becoming involved with a man who misrepresented himself as a bachelor. Months later I learned that he had a wife and three children in an upstate New York town. When my first shock and pain faded, I found that it was my self-esteem, rather than my heart, that had suffered the most. But Aunt Ellen persisted in a belief that I was just "putting a brave face on things," and that underneath I was utterly crushed. In fact I was sure that she had organized this European trip, the first for any of the three of us, mainly as a form of emotional therapy for me.

She was saying, "I don't want anything to spoil things for her."

"Now how can Guy Nordeen spoil things?"

"Oh, Brad! By keeping her reminded of what happened to her mother, that's how. You know that in all these years she's almost never asked questions about her mother. And that isn't normal, Brad. It means she's never gotten over it."

She paused, and then burst out, "And I wish he weren't so darned good-looking. Especially after what that dreadful man did to her feelings, she might find herself attracted to a man like Guy Nordeen. And that would set up an awful conflict."

Uncle Brad groaned. "Good lord, Ellie. They haven't met, and probably never will. Venice is a pretty big town. And yet in your imagination Linda is already in love with him, and maybe married to him, and so miserable that they're all five going to shrinks—"

"All five?"

"Sure. While you're dreaming up disasters, you might as well dream up triplets for them."

"You can joke. Just the same, I have this feeling—"

"You and your feelings."

"I have this feeling that we ought not to wait another two weeks before we go to Florence. We ought to go tomorrow morning."

"And camp out in some piazza until we can claim our hotel reservations? This is the height of the season in Italy, remember."

After I'd heard so much, I couldn't walk out onto my own balcony. It would be too embarrassing for all of us. Moving softly through the gloom, I took a pale blue cotton dress from the armoire, elaborately carved and perhaps genuinely antique, which served as a clothes closet. In the bathroom I turned on the light and took a shower and dressed. Then I stood in front of the washbasin mirror, brushing my hair.

I wear my blond hair short. My mother's hair reached below her shoulders. But I know, from memory as well as old photographs, that otherwise I look very much like her. The same gray eyes and high cheekbones, the same wide mouth and rather square jaw. As I looked at my mirrored face, so like that of a woman who had died

4

when not many years older than I was now, I realized that Aunt Ellen was right. I had never recovered from my loss.

And that, of course, was not normal. For a young child, the shock of a parent's death, even a violent death, ultimately grows dim. But my memories of the events seventeen years ago held something more than loss, something evil, nameless, and yet very real to me. Sometimes, as now, when I looked at the mirrored face that almost might have been my mother's, I had a sense of that evil, swirling invisibly in the air behind me. . . .

I laid my brush down on the marble shelf beside the washbasin, turned out the bathroom light and slipped out into the hall.

Downstairs, I walked through the luxurious lobby with its forest of highly polished black marble pillars and then out onto the broad terrace overlooking the Grand Canal. Few of the tables under the pastel-colored umbrellas were occupied. It was still a little early for most of the aperitif crowd. I sat down at a table near the hotel's pink stucco facade, ordered a Campari and soda, and gazed out over the water to the Church of San Giorgio Maggiore on its private island. Sunset was about two hours away, but already the light had taken on a bronze tinge, warming the centuries-old brick of the church's campanile.

From the Piazza San Marco, only a stone's throw from where I sat, came the sound of the giant bronze Moors in the Clock Tower striking five o'clock. That meant that an hour, or close to it, would pass before Aunt Ellen and Uncle Brad came down to the terrace. I was glad that I would have a little more time to myself. That overheard conversation had upset me. It shouldn't have, I realized. Aunt Ellen's fears were groundless. Even if I met this Guy Nordeen, I would not fall for him, no matter how good-looking he turned out to be. It was unthinkable that I could feel attracted to anyone who lived in that Connecticut town. And yet there was this odd unease . . .

6

I became aware that a man was watching me.

He sat alone at a table near the terrace's western balustrade. Because the lowering sun was behind him, I could not see his face clearly, but he was blond. I also gained an impression that he was young, probably in his late twenties. I saw him look away, then look back at me. I turned my head so that I was facing out over the water, but I could still see him from the corner of my eye. He beckoned a waiter. The waiter looked toward me, said something to the blond man.

He was coming toward me now, tall and easy-moving in white duck trousers and a black-and-white striped jersey. Guy Nordeen, the man Aunt Ellen and Uncle Brad had been discussing? Somehow I was sure of it.

My pulse, as if with some foreknowledge of all that this meeting would bring me, had increased its pace. He said, "Miss Edwards?"

"Yes." Aunt Ellen had been right about him. He was good-looking, devastatingly so. One lock of his slightly curling blond hair fell across his tanned forehead. His eyes were a deep sea blue, his nose straight, his mouth wide with a sensually full lower lip, his chin square but without that heavy aggressiveness one associates with football linemen and Central American dictators. Most women, I was sure, must feel a mixed reaction upon meeting him—physical attraction mingled with a warning sense that any man that handsome could not be trusted.

"My name is Guy Nordeen. As you probably guessed, I asked the waiter who you were. Nervy, I'll admit. But maybe you'll forgive me when I tell you that I know your uncle. I mean, the waiter also told me that you were staying here with your uncle and aunt, Mr. and Mrs. Bradford Cartwright."

"They're not really my aunt and uncle."

Now why had I said that? My relationship to the Cartwrights was something I seldom explained to acquaintances, and never to someone I'd met only seconds before.

He frowned. "But the waiter said—" He broke off. "Would you mind if I sat down?"

I did mind, very much. But I heard myself saying, "Please do."

When he had taken the white wrought-iron chair opposite mine, I said, "My father was Mr. Cartwright's cousin. After my mother died—I was six then—the Cartwrights adopted me."

I had a brief, bleak memory of my small self standing in the living room of that house in the woods near Wessex. Gray light fell through a north window onto the sparse furnishings, and onto the easel that my mother had said belonged to my father, and onto the compassionate face of the woman I was to know as Aunt Ellen. She knelt and drew me into her arms.

I have no memory of attending my mother's funeral. Although I never asked Aunt Ellen about it, I'm fairly sure that she did not take me to it. In my next memory of those days I was in a car seated between Ellen and Bradford Cartwright, traveling toward New York. They were going to adopt me, she said. (She did not explain that I had no other blood relatives, none at all.) I was to call them aunt and uncle.

To this day I don't know why she didn't ask me to call her Mummy, or Mama Ellen, or some other version of the word "mother." Maybe she thought I might not want to. Maybe she thought it would only serve to keep me reminded of the loss of my real mother.

"So that's it," Guy Nordeen said. "It's not surprising to hear that you're not closely related to them. You don't look like either of the Cartwrights."

Those very blue eyes, lingering on my face, told me that he liked what he was seeing. I felt pleased and yet dismayed by my pleasure.

"Do you live with the Cartwrights in Manhattan?"

"In Manhattan, but not with the Cartwrights. Since I graduated from Barnard, I've lived in a loft in SoHo."

"Painter? Writer? Clothes designer?"

"Painter, of a sort. I do book jackets."

"You like that?"

"Yes. I have no illusions about my talent. I'll never be exhibited in Fifty-seventh Street galleries. But it's nice to be able to make a living from what talent I have."

Why was I chattering on about myself? I asked, "How long have you known Uncle Brad?"

"A couple of years, ever since he did some legal work for my family's firm in Connecticut." I knew that Uncle Brad, a moderately successful lawyer, had been hired from time to time by Connecticut business establishments. "We have an importing firm in Hartford."

Hartford? Hopefully I wondered if Aunt Ellen and Uncle Brad had been mistaken. Perhaps this man had no connection with Wessex.

"Do you live in Hartford?"

"No. For about a hundred years my family has lived in Wessex, a very old town on the Connecticut River. It's an easy commute from Hartford."

So he did live in that town whose very name repelled me, even though I could not recall the look of a single one of its streets or a single building.

He asked, "What's your hometown?"

9

I couldn't answer that truthfully. Doing so would have evoked questions, questions I could not answer without speaking of my mother's lonely death in that woodland pond. And I did not want to discuss that with this handsome stranger, here on a sun-flooded Venetian terrace.

"I was raised in Manhattan," I said evasively. I asked, before he could speak, "Where did you meet Uncle Brad and Aunt Ellen? Here in Venice, I mean?"

"At a glass factory over on the island of Murano. Your uncle mentioned that they were staying at this hotel, and so late this afternoon I decided to drop by here, in the hope I might find them having drinks here on the terrace."

I had known Uncle Brad and Aunt Ellen were taking the glass factory tour to Murano. Because I didn't relish the idea of being herded with a crowd of other tourists in and out of buildings, I had chosen to wander alone through the heat and midday hush of Venice.

"Among other things," Guy Nordeen said, "our firm imports Venetian glass. Hence this business trip." He grinned. "Although before I came here I managed to get in some sunning and snorkeling along the Italian Riviera."

He added, looking toward the hotel entrance, "Here come the Cartwrights now."

Even from yards away I could see the dismay in Aunt Ellen's face at sight of my companion. I saw, too, the I-told-you-so look she flashed at her husband. But by the time they reached the table, she had reassumed her usual pleasant manner. She made no objection when Guy Nordeen signaled the waiter and ordered drinks for all of us.

Later, when Guy suggested that we four dine at the Quadri, Aunt Ellen looked at me hopefully. It was obvious she wanted me to make some excuse for refusing. I did not. Oh, I knew that I should. But everything around me—the water now dyed with saffron and rose, the bright flowers blooming in cement boxes along the balustrades, the attractive-looking people at the other tables, and the superlatively handsome one at our own—all of that seemed to have cast a spell upon me.

We dined on crab at the Quadri. Later, we sat at one of the tables in the vast Piazza San Marco, sipping coffee and listening to a gaudily uniformed band play the sort of music—"O Solo Mio" and "Pines of Rome," and the "Habanera" from *Carmen*—that had beguiled generations of visitors to Venice. Again my surroundings—the enormous square itself, and the tall Clock Tower, and the oriental-domed Basilica of St. Mark, all bathed in the amber glow of floodlights—brought me a sense of enchantment, so strong that even though I was sure that this smiling young man could bring me to disaster, I could not turn away from him. When, under cover of the music, he asked me to have lunch with him the next day, I said, "Thank you. I will."

A few minutes after the Cartwrights and I had returned to our hotel, Aunt Ellen tapped on my door. Inside my room, she sat down on the dressing-table bench and said, "I have to ask you, Linda. Do you know where that young man is from?"

"Yes, he told me. Wessex, Connecticut."

She looked at me for a long, troubled moment. Obviously she wanted to ask more questions, but feared to tread upon what was very delicate ground indeed. At last she said, "He's very attractive."

"Yes."

"But I hope you won't rush into anything, Linda. An

experience like yours with that awful Eberle person can leave a girl—vulnerable."

Joe Eberle was the name of the philandering married man I'd fallen for. "Vulnerable to what? Guy Nordeen will be here only two or three days longer. He told us so at dinner, remember? And even if he weren't leaving, we'll be going to Florence before long. And that will be the end of it."

For several seconds she sat there in troubled silence. Then she said, with seeming irrelevance, "We feel you are just as much our daughter as if you'd been born to us."

I looked with love and gratitude into her face, with the youthfully snub nose that made her gray-sprinkled dark hair look incongruous. Then I crossed the room and kissed her cheek. "Don't worry, Aunt Ellen. There's nothing to worry about."

But there was. Guy did not leave Venice. Saying vaguely that his plans had changed, he stayed on at his hotel on the Grand Canal's left bank, making short business trips to towns like Udine and Padua but always returning to Venice before nightfall. He and I dined among noisily exuberant Americans at Harry's Bar and even more noisy Italians at small trattorias. We attended a performance of Moliere's *Misanthrope* at Teatro La Fenice, that small jewel box of a theater. One afternoon, we took the steamer along the Brenta Canal, past poplars and weeping willows, past the Palladian palaces to which, in past centuries, the Venetian rich had retired in summer.

At night, lying awake, I would wonder if Aunt Ellen was right. Perhaps my ego-damaging experience with Joe Eberle had left me more vulnerable. Certainly I found it impossible to deny myself Guy Nordeen's company. I couldn't even bring myself to tell him that I had misled him about my place of birth, lest such a confession lower his opinion of me.

THE SIXTH day after we met, Guy hired a motorboat. In shorts and T-shirts, we skimmed out over a lagoon, which sparkled in the late-morning sun. He knew a small deserted island on the far side of the lagoon, Guy said. Well away from the steamer routes between the inhabited islands, it would be a fine place for a picnic.

We reached it, an irregularly shaped bit of land that measured only about two hundred yards across at its widest point. A mooring post stood beside the decaying little wharf. On the island's far side, the ruins of what might have been a shed and animal pens rose above the long, green-brown grass. Apparently, Guy said, some farmer had once grazed sheep or goats here.

I said, "I wonder why he stopped."

"The island shrunk too much, I guess. All the islands in the lagoon are being eaten away by the tides."

We brought a blanket and the picnic hamper ashore. Guy spread the blanket on the grass at the dock's edge. We stretched out. Eyes closed, skin warmed by the sunlight, I listened to the silence. No, not complete silence. There was the whisper of wind through the long grass. And there were faint, plopping sounds. After a moment I realized what the sounds meant. Bits of the island's soft earth were falling into the water. So even as we lay here, the island was shrinking, shrinking.

All of a sudden I wished time could stop. Right then, with Guy Nordeen beside me, and sunlight drenching my body, and the whisper of wind in my ears. The very sound of bits of the island breaking away, so remindful that all things must change, only made the perfection of the moment more poignant.

I sensed that he was watching me. I opened my eyes. He lay propped on one elbow, blond hair glinting in the sun, his very blue, very serious eyes fixed on my face.

He leaned closer and kissed me. We'd kissed before, of course, and each time I'd been stirred by the touch of that warm mouth with its full underlip, but never so much so as now.

He raised his head. "I love you," he said.

And I loved him, loved him as I hadn't known anyone could love. But I must not say so.

"I want to marry you, Linda."

Unable to speak, I shook my head.

"Why not?" he asked, almost harshly. "I thought you were—growing fond of me."

Fond of him! I said nothing, but he must have read my thoughts in my eyes, because he said, smiling now, "Is it just that I'm going too fast for you? Is that it?"

"No. It's that I can't marry you, ever."

"For God's sake, Linda! What is it? Some other man?"

"No. There was a man, someone I met last summer. But I never loved him. I know that now."

"How do you know it now? How do you know you didn't love that other man?" His voice was sternly triumphant. "You do love me, don't you?"

Helpless, I just looked up at him. He said, in a roughened voice, "I know you do. It's in your face."

He thrust one arm under me, gathered me close, brought his lips down on mine. His other hand slipped under my T-shirt, cupped my breast, then reached around me to unfasten my bra.

For a moment I almost gave way to the desire awakened by his lips and the feel of his big warm hand against my skin. Then I began to fight both myself and him. I wrenched my lips free, beat the palm of one hand against his shoulder.

He released me. I sat up. Face averted, I rested my head on my updrawn knees.

After perhaps a minute he said, "It wasn't just lust. Oh, not that I don't want you. My God, yes. But I guess I felt that afterward you might feel you had to make an honest man of me."

I could tell he had meant the words to sound light, but they hadn't come out that way. I turned my head to look at him. He too was sitting up now, his face rather pale beneath its tan.

He said, "Don't you think you owe me some sort of explanation?"

There was no help for it now. "Yes," I said and then blurted out the first words that came into my head. "I lied to you, or the same as lied. New York wasn't my birthplace. I was born in Wessex."

He looked astounded. "Wessex? Wessex, Connecticut?"

"Yes. I guess you never heard of a Linda Edwards there."

He said, still with that bewildered look, "No. And Edwards is such a common name."

Besides, as we both knew now, he was almost five years

16

my senior. In childhood, five years is an enormous gap. There was little chance that he, an upper-class boy who had gone away to boarding school when he was nine, would be aware of a little girl, a preschooler, in an isolated house outside the village limits.

"Where did you live in Wessex? Who was your father?"

I almost welcomed the chance to tell him about my father. It meant I could delay for a moment talking of my mother's death.

"His name was George Edwards, and he was a commercial artist, like me, except that he did mainly posters and calendars and so on." Often I had reflected how he, the father I couldn't remember, had bequeathed me my small but salable talent.

"He died when I was not quite three. He was killed in the crash of a small commercial plane that carried passengers between southern Connecticut and La Guardia. He was on his way to see a New York greeting card publisher when it happened."

"That must have been rough. I'm sorry."

"I don't even remember him," I said. "And anyway, it probably pleased him to know, if he did know, that he was leaving my mother and me fairly well provided for. We were able to go on living in the same house. It was my mother's house, inherited from my grandmother. My mother didn't have to work, although when I was five she did start to make extra money. There was this grocery store owned by a woman named Dilsey, who'd been a friend of my grandmother's—"

"Dilsey Wolsifer? She's still in Wessex. She runs a bakery."

"Well, she had a grocery store then. I'm almost sure of

it. Anyway, my mother had always like to collect things in the woods—mushrooms and wild berries and edible greens. She started selling them to Dilsey."

I broke off, looking out over the water to where the domes and towers of Venice glinted in the sun. I was getting close to the nightmarish part now.

Guy asked, "What was your mother's name?"

"Charity Craig Edwards. She drowned when I was six."

I saw a flicker in his eyes and knew he must have suddenly remembered at least something about what had happened one summer night when he was not quite eleven and I had just turned six.

He said, in a reluctant voice, "Wasn't there some question for a while about whether—"

"Yes." Now that I had started, I found that the words came out more easily than I had expected them to. "There was the question of whether she'd—she'd slipped into that pool by accident, or had deliberately thrown herself in, or—or had been—"

"I remember now," Guy said quickly. "I remember grown-ups talking about it, and even other kids. But I went back to boarding school for the fall term, and by next summer everyone had forgotten about it."

I heard another chunk of soft earth fall into the water. Then I said, "The night that it happened, I woke up in my room. I was afraid, but with no idea why I was afraid."

Now that I'd finally begun to tell him about it, the words tumbled out of me. "The room was full of moonlight, almost as bright as day—"

I went on, telling him how I had left my small bed and, barefoot, had run down the darker hallway to my

18

mother's room. The door was open. Her bed was empty, the covers neatly turned back. My nameless fear grew, like something swelling within me, cutting off my breath. I heard myself crying, "Mama!"

No answer. I crossed the hall to the bathroom. No one. I went down the dark, steep staircase, almost tripping once on my nightgown, and emerged into the living room, also filled with that blue-white moonlight. Not pausing, I turned and fled back through the kitchen and down the short hall beyond. I opened a closed door and cried, "Sara!"

Sara Breed, who helped Mama with the housework and cooking and took care of me sometimes when Mama went to the village alone. Kind, coarse-featured Sara, who had threads of gray in her black hair, and yet who, I'd somehow sensed, wasn't really grown up in her mind—in fact, not much older than myself.

Mama, too, seemed to feel that Sara wasn't a real grown-up. For instance, Sara often slipped out of the house at night to wander in the woods. Mama would scold her about it in much the same tone in which she scolded me when I did something dangerous, such as try to walk on the split-rail fence that bounded our yard.

Sara's bed also was empty. I remembered then. It was Wednesday, and every Wednesday night, after supper, Sara left to spend two days at her aunt's house on the other side of Wessex.

But where had Mama gone? Was she walking in the woods? She often did that in the daytime. Of course, it was night now, but on such a bright night . . .

I sped back through the living room, tugged the front door open, went out onto the roofless little porch. Ahead was the grassy clearing in which the old house stood. It was bisected by a brick-paved path, with marigolds blooming on either side of it, their yellow blossoms dyed bluish by the moonlight.

Dimly aware that the brick path was cool and rough to my bare feet, I ran about halfway to the dark stand of trees at the clearing's far edge. Then I stopped, almost as if I'd run into some invisible obstacle.

As I stood motionless, I became aware of more than fear. I had a sense of some nameless evil, powerful and implacable, something that had taken Mama and now might take me. It seemed to pulse in the moon-drenched air, like a gigantic heart.

For a few seconds I stood paralyzed. Then, like a small animal bolting to its den, I fled back into the house, up the narrow dark stairs. In my bed I pulled the covers up over my head and sobbed with bewildered terror. Now and then I would call, "Mama!" but there was never any answer, just the silent house, and, outside it, that terrible pulsing something. . . .

At last I must have fallen into exhausted sleep, because suddenly I opened my eyes to see a man standing beside my bed, his thin, middle-aged face sorrowful in the early sunlight coming through the window. Mr. Walsh—Officer Walsh—who on summer weekends often directed traffic on Main Street. "Better get dressed, little lady, and come downstairs."

He went out. I dressed, buckling my sandals carefully, as if by doing that task right I could make everything all right. Just as I reached the foot of the stairs, the front door opened, and Dilsey Wolsifer came in. Dilsey, who'd been my grandmother's best friend. She said, looking down at me, "Oh, my little Linda."

It was then that I knew my mother was not coming back, ever.

"There's a gap in my memory after that," I said, looking out over the lagoon. The sun was well past its zenith now, and its reflections in the water had taken on a warmer tint. "Maybe I stayed with Dilsey Wolsifer for a few days. More likely, she stayed with me at my house. Anyway, my next memory is of Aunt Ellen and Uncle Brad in that living room, telling me that I was to be their little girl."

Another gap after that. Then the memory of riding through streets lined with buildings higher than any I had ever seen. This was New York, Uncle Brad said, and I was going to live here.

I stopped speaking. After a while Guy said, "How did you learn—what had happened?"

"To my mother? I don't know. I just know that even before Uncle Brad and Aunt Ellen took me away from Wessex I'd learned, probably from overheard conversation, that she'd been found in the pool below the waterfall. It was our pool. Oh, I don't mean that it was on land we owned. But we often had picnic lunches down there. My mother loved picnics. We'd sit on that footbridge above the pool with our legs dangling."

Again I fell silent. Guy said, "I'm beginning to remember more about it now. Wasn't someone—indicted? Some woman your mother employed?"

"Yes. Sara Breed. Months after my mother died, Sara went to the police and confessed. But I didn't know about her confession for a long time, around five years. I found these clippings—"

It had happened, I told Guy, one winter Saturday when I was almost eleven. Aunt Ellen, who had flu, was confined to her bedroom in our rambling apartment on East Seventy-second Street. In my role as nurse, I bustled importantly between the bedroom and her bathroom and the kitchen, where I prepared such sickroom delicacies as stewed oysters and orange juice with an egg beaten up in it. Late in the afternoon, my aunt asked me to bring her appointment book from her desk in the room we rather grandly called the library, although it was also the TV room and Uncle Brad's study.

In the big corner room, with snow falling past the windows, I walked to Aunt Ellen's desk, a small one against a wall. I opened the lower left-hand drawer and went through its contents. No appointment book. But beneath everything else I found a large manila envelope with the words "Charity Craig Edwards" written on it in Aunt Ellen's neat hand.

Charity Craig Edwards, my mother.

Suddenly I no longer seemed to be in this safe, comfortable apartment where I had lived for almost five years. Instead I was all alone back in that old house, with moonlight flooding through the windows. . . .

I knew instinctively that Aunt Ellen had not meant for me to see the contents of this envelope, whatever they were, at least not yet. She must have forgotten the envelope was in this drawer. Or perhaps she had told me to look in the *right*-hand drawer.

I laid the envelope on the desk top, opened the lower right drawer. There was the appointment book. I took it to Aunt Ellen. I said, as she riffled through it, "May I go to my room for a while?"

She looked at me over the granny glasses perched on her little nose. "Of course, dear. I'm fine. Besides, your Uncle Brad will be home soon."

I returned to the library and, heart beating fast, carried the manila envelope to my own pretty room, with its white furniture and blue flocked wall paper. Inside the envelope were several newspaper clippings, each of which Aunt Ellen had marked with the words, *Hartford Courier Sentinel,* plus a date. There was also a thick blue document in a blue cover. "Court Transcript," the blue cover said, and under that, "Sara Breed versus the State of Connecticut."

Sara, my friend, who'd been more like me than a grown-up.

I opened the transcript. Right at the beginning there was a long paragraph, filled with phrases like "Whereas having sworn" and "deponent alleges." Dismayed, I laid the transcript aside. I would never make sense of that, at least not before Uncle Brad got home. Better to read the clippings.

I sorted them out by dates. The first one, dated August 17 of that summer almost five years in the past, was headlined WIDOW FOUND DROWNED. The story began, "The body of Charity Craig Edwards, 34, a resident of Wessex, Connecticut, was found face down this morning in a woodland pool near this fashionable small village. A fisherman found the body. It is reported that Mrs. Edwards, a widow, was the mother of a six-year-old daughter. Police are investigating."

Still with that chill sense that time had turned backward, I went on to the next clipping, dated two days later. It said that an autopsy had revealed that my mother, a few hours prior to her death, had taken a large number of sleeping pills.

I thought, *why?* Had she left me of her own free will, my loving and so beloved mother? Had she taken the pills, and then walked through the woods in her summer nightgown, with blue-white moonlight filtering through the trees—

No! Here in my pretty room, five years and more than a hundred miles away from that night, I was passionately sure that she hadn't gone into that pool of her own accord.

I read the news story's final sentence: "Mrs. Edwards is to be buried in the Presbyterian churchyard in Wessex." Then, hands shaking, I lifted that clipping and looked at the one underneath.

Its headline was: HOUSEMAID CONFESSES TO MURDER OF HER EMPLOYER. Under the dateline of October 15, the story went on to say that Sara Breed, 32, had walked into the Wessex, Connecticut, police station the day before and confessed to having murdered her employer, Charity Craig Edwards, the previous August. "Miss Breed, who was employed by the slain woman as cook and housemaid, stated that she had mixed a barbiturate with every item of food and drink she had served to Mrs. Edwards at dinner that night. Later she had roused the almost unconscious woman and half led, half dragged her to a natural pool a half mile from the house. There she drew her into the water and held her head beneath the surface until she stopped struggling.

"Miss Breed, Wessex authorities say, was diagnosed when a child as mildly retarded. Orphaned soon after her birth, she was adopted and raised by an aunt.

"Police say the woman has not disclosed the motive for her act. The district attorney's office is investigating, and an early indictment is expected."

Some mistake, I thought, feeling sick. Sara had loved both my mother and me. And although she hadn't been bright, she certainly hadn't seemed in the least crazy.

I looked at the last clipping, dated three months after the previous one. Under the headline WOMAN

24

JUDGED NOT GUILTY AFTER ATTORNEY'S IN-SANITY PLEA, the story went on, "Sara Breed, arrested last October as the self-confessed slayer of a Wessex, Connecticut, widow, Charity Edwards, was found not guilty by reason of insanity yesterday in a Hartford courtroom. Throughout her trial, when questioned about the reason for her act, Miss Breed replied that she did not know. She gave the same response whenever she was asked where she had obtained the barbiturates which figured in the case.

"Miss Breed has been remanded to the custody of the State Hospital for the Criminally Insane at Claverly, Connecticut."

So that was what had happened to Sara. Although the jury had said, "Not guilty," she still had been put behind bars.

My head jerked up. A muffled sound out in the apartment-house hallway. The elevator door opened and closed. In a few seconds I might hear Uncle Brad's key in the lock. I stuffed the transcript and the newspaper clippings back into the envelope, carried it swiftly back to the library and replaced it in the lower left-hand drawer of Aunt Ellen's desk.

Silent now, arms encircling my updrawn knees, I watched a long-legged bird—some sort of heron?—dive into the lagoon and then fly off with a flapping fish in its beak. Guy asked, "Did you ever tell the Cartwrights you'd found that envelope?"

"Never."

After a moment he said, "I wonder why she'd saved the transcript and the news stories."

"For me, I suppose. I mean, she must have thought that someday I would ask her what had happened after

25

they took me away from Wessex. If by that time she had judged me old enough to understand, she'd have had those things to show me. But I never did ask."

I remembered Aunt Ellen saying on the balcony outside their hotel room, "In all these years she hasn't talked about her mother. And that isn't normal, Brad."

I could feel Guy's intent gaze on my face. "I can realize how rough it must have been for a six-year-old kid," he said. "Your father was already gone. And then to lose your mother, especially in  that way. The very thankfulness I feel that both my parents are still alive and still together helps me know what your mother's death must have meant to you."

He paused, and then burst out, "But that was a long time ago. Why does it have anything to do with us?"

"Because it's still back there, whatever I felt that night."

"Linda!"

"I'm certain. It's still there, that—that threatening thing I felt throbbing all around me when I ran out of the house that night. If I go back there—"

"For God's sake, darling. You were a kid, a terrified little kid who'd waked up to find herself all alone in an isolated house. No wonder you had a sense of something threatening you. But that's no reason why, all these years later, you should refuse to marry me."

I turned my face toward him. "It is! Even if it's—all in my mind, it's still very real to me. Real enough that I couldn't go back there, even with you."

His eyes, so deeply blue against the golden tan of his face, studied me for a long moment. Then he said quietly, "All right. You don't have to go back. There are lots of other places we could live."

26

I shook my head. "Your people have lived in Wessex for almost a century. I can't be the reason for your—exiling yourself."

"But if I'm willing to—"

"You're willing now. But later, when things went wrong, and things do go wrong in any marriage, you'd blame our troubles on me, for having uprooted you." As he started to speak, I said swiftly, "This isn't a spur-of-the-moment reaction. I started thinking about it days ago, from the first moment I realized that we might become serious about each other."

He was silent for perhaps a minute. Then he asked, "Is that your last word?"

Wretchedly, I nodded.

After a while, his gaze left my face. He said, looking at the picnic hamper beside us on the grass, "Would you like some lunch now?"

"No, thanks. I think I'd better go back to the hotel."

"All right. I'm not hungry either."

He gathered up the hamper and the blanket. Just before I stepped into the hired motorboat, I looked across the lagoon at Venice. By some trick of the afternoon light, the city with its rosy campaniles and gold-capped domes seemed to float above the water, unreal as a dream. Irrelevantly, I wondered if Shakespeare, before he wrote his "insubstantial pageant" speech—"the cloud-capped towers, the gorgeous palaces"—had seen Venice from about this distance on a summer's day. But, for me, what had proved "insubstantial" was the hope, thin at best, that I could go on seeing this man and yet escape profound hurt, both to him and myself.

We said almost nothing during the trip back across the lagoon. At the hotel landing, he tied the boat to one of the striped mooring piles and then helped me onto the dock.

He said, "I guess there's nothing more to say." His eyes were as miserable as I knew mine must be.

"I guess not." And yet I stood waiting for him to say something additional. "Good-bye," I said finally, "good luck," and turned away.

Aunt Ellen and Uncle Brad and I took the train to Florence two days later. During those two days Guy did not appear at the hotel, nor did he call, even though I went about tense with the expectation of seeing him on the street, or of hearing the desk clerk say, "Oh, Miss Edwards. A Mr. Nordeen called while you were out." By the time the luggage-laden water taxi left the Cartwrights and me at the railroad station, I was sure that Guy was already back on the other side of the Atlantic.

## FOUR

I HATED Florence. The place was too hot, I told myself. The sidewalks were too narrow, and the winding medieval streets too clogged with noisy traffic. At the Uffizi, the galleries were so jammed with chattering tourists that you couldn't see the pictures.

But I knew that right then I wasn't even interested in the pictures. The trouble wasn't with Florence. The trouble was my own unhappiness. I knew now that I loved Guy as I probably never would love anyone again. And I had thrown away all he offered me.

I should have agreed to marry him, I felt now. Yes, even if it had meant that sooner or later I would find myself back in that town where I'd been born. After all, I couldn't even name the menace that, in my mind, the town seemed to hold. And yet because of that fear I had lost the handsome, well-born young man who loved me.

On our third afternoon in Florence we "did" the Palazzo Vecchio, Florence's medieval city hall, and its courtyard adorned with statues by Verrocchio and Cellini. As the guide droned on about some young fifteenth-century thug named Pazzi who had murdered a Medici, I thought viciously, "Who cares who stabbed who five hundred years ago?" When we crossed to the straw market, and the guide pointed out the bronze boar whose nose people for generations had stroked for good luck, I looked at the boar's shiny snout and thought, "Who cares?"

His voice was low and almost hoarse. "Linda."

I whirled around. It seemed to me that the handsome face was thinner than it had appeared a few days before. "Guy!" I neither knew nor cared whether the Cartwrights, backs turned to me as they listened to the guide, heard my voice. "Oh, darling!"

Joy leaped into his face. He grasped my arm, led me around one of the straw market stalls and then a few feet down a narrow cobblestoned street. We went into each other's arms and kissed, a long, long kiss.

I said, "I thought you'd gone home."

"I meant to, but I couldn't. Finally I knew that I had to follow you here. Listen, my dearest. I'll never ask you to set foot in Wessex. And I'll never reproach you because we are living someplace else. I swear it."

"We'll live in Wessex, where you belong! Oh, darling, how could I have been such a fool? Why should I be afraid of anything, especially my own childish imaginings, when I'll have you to keep me safe?"

WE DROVE into Wessex about an hour before sunset on a warm day in mid-October.

The apprehension I felt was mild, surely not much more than any bride might feel at the prospect of meeting her in-laws for the first time. After the blissful weeks just past, I had a sense of being one of Fortune's darlings, safe from almost anything, let alone a shadow in my mind.

In Florence, thanks to the American consul, Guy had been able to cut swiftly through Italian red tape and obtain a marriage license. The ceremony, with the Cartwrights as our only witnesses, was in an unexpectedly drab room—no Renaissance murals on the walls; just gray paint and a photograph of Florence's current mayor—in the Palazzo Vecchio, the ancient city hall. But I couldn't have been happier if the air had throbbed with Mendelssohn and a half-dozen bridesmaids had preceded me down a beribboned aisle to a flower-banked altar.

Almost immediately after the ceremony, the Cartwrights and Guy and I had boarded the train to Rome. That evening Guy and I caught a plane for the Caribbean. After five sun-soaked weeks on an island so small that it doesn't even appear on some maps, we flew

31

to New York, where we shared several meals with my aunt and uncle, saw a few shows, and had a tag sale of most of the furnishings of my loft before turning the place back to the landlord. Guy reclaimed his yellow Mustang from the long-term parking lot at Kennedy, where he had left it all those weeks ago before flying to Italy for what he had expected to be a fairly short business trip. Then we drove east and north across a Connecticut warmed by an almost summerlike sun, but with trees here and there touched by autumn red or gold.

We turned off the interstate at an exit marked "Wessex" and drove for several miles along a narrower road bordered by mingled pines and deciduous trees. We passed a lake where stately white swans floated among squawking, wing-flapping Canadian geese. The road began to wind gently past fine old frame houses, some with Victorian turrets and cupolas, some with the classic pitched roofs and tiny porches of the Federalist period, some with the narrow clapboards and tiny-paned windows of the eighteenth century.

Then we were in the town's business district. Handsome shops, many with the logos of famous Fifth Avenue stores on their plate-glass windows, lined both sides of the street. We rounded a curve. I gasped. The street, sloping here, ended at a wharf extending out into the broad Connecticut River. I saw sparkling water, sleek power cruisers, sailing yachts with canvas tinged by sunset pink.

Without my asking him to, Guy eased over to the curb and stopped. "Nice, huh? Every time I come back here from a trip, I'm struck all over again by that view. And just think. Boats of various kinds have been tying up at that spot for the last three hundred and fifty years, ever since Indians brought canoe-loads of deer and beaver hides to trade with the first white settlers."

Had I seen that wharf as a child? In all probability. I knew I had sometimes gone shopping with my mother in the village. But I had no memory of seeing the broad river, and the wharf, and the swaying masts of sleek yachts.

We were still gazing at the river when, from the corner of my eye, I saw a woman open the door of a shop and step out onto the sidewalk. "Guy! Guy Nordeen!"

"Peggy!"

Swiftly he swung the car door open, got out, and kissed her cheek soundly. "Love, here's someone I want you to know."

She smiled at me. "Don't tell me. Let me guess. It's Mrs. Guy Nordeen, the third."

He said, "So you heard."

"The whole town has heard."

She was a fine-boned brunette with classic features and with a striking streak of gray running back from a widow's peak. As she stood there, Gucci shopping bag in hand, she seemed the embodiment of country chic—suit of soft-looking brown suede, beige cowl-necked blouse of some sort of silky knit, set off by a chunky bronze pin with a one-of-a-kind look. Age? I guessed a well-exercised, carefully dieted forty-five. Whatever her age, she was an attractive woman indeed.

Guy said, "Peggy, this is Linda. Linda, this is Peggy Crofton. Better be nice to her. She runs this town."

"Don't believe a word of it," she said. "My, aren't you pretty! Welcome to Wessex, Linda. I hope we're going to be good friends."

"I hope so, too."

"On guard, Linda," Guy said. "That means she wants to put you to work. Friends of the Library. Garden Club. Animal Protection League. Ladies' Village society—"

33

"Guy, stop it!" Her dark eyes turned to me. "We're not going to overwork Linda. Everyone's heard that she is an artist."

"Only in a way. I do book jackets."

"Don't be modest. I'm sure it takes quite a lot of talent to produce an acceptable book jacket."

As a matter of fact, I agreed with that statement, but could scarcely say so.

Peggy went on, "Just the same, I hope you'll find time to join the Ladies' Village Society. Sorry about that 'ladies.' It was founded back in the days when 'women' was considered an impolite word."

"I'd be glad to join," I said, even though I wasn't sure I would, just as I wasn't sure I liked Peggy Crofton, in spite of her cordiality.

Guy said, "Drop you off at your house?"

"No, darling. I have a little more shopping to do. Besides, walking is good for the figure." She laid one thin hand on his arm. "So very good to have you back."

I stiffened. Now I knew why I hadn't been sure I liked her. There was no mistaking the faint huskiness in her voice, or the way they smiled into each other's eyes. Guy and this woman, so much older than himself, had been lovers. When, I didn't know. I just knew that they had.

She turned toward me. "Good-bye, Linda. I'll be calling you soon."

Hoping that she could not see my discovery in my face, I managed some sort of reply.

She walked away up the street. Guy got behind the wheel and started the engine. As we moved away from the curb he said, "Quite a gal, that Peggy."

"Have you known her long?"

"For as long as I can remember."

"Then she was born here?"

"No, somewhere in Massachusetts. She came here after she married Hal Crofton. That must have been about twenty-five years ago."

"Is Hal Crofton rich?" I was thinking of the designer suit, the handmade pin.

We had turned off the main street onto one that paralleled the river. On the right, more fine old houses stood among trees on sloping lawns.

"*Was* rich," Guy answered, "far and away the richest man in town. He shot himself to death twenty-odd years ago."

"Shot himself! Why?"

"Unsound mind, the coroner's jury said. And apparently he'd always been something of an oddball. Had never worked. Hadn't needed to. His grandfather, a Boston banker, had left him a trust fund, which had grown enormously by the time Hal Crofton received it."

"If he didn't work, what did he do?"

"Tinkered with clocks, like that poor fat Louis, Marie Antoinette's husband. It's funny how often eccentrics go in for clocks. I don't imagine the townspeople respected him much, in spite of all his money. Not that I remember much about the whole thing. I was still quite small when he killed himself."

After a moment Guy added, "You've certainly got to give Peggy credit. Especially in a small town, there's always a stigma attached to being the wife or husband of a suicide. Peggy could have gone anywhere in the world to escape the talk. Instead she stuck it out here and lived the whole thing down and became what she is now." He turned right again, onto an upward sloping street.

"Just what is she now?"

35

If my voice had held a jealous edge, apparently he hadn't heard it. He answered, "I wasn't kidding when I said she runs this town. The mayor and the board of trustees, for instance, would never dream of allowing a new advertising sign on Main Street if Peggy's Village Society disapproved of it."

He swung the car into a long driveway. "Well, there it is, my darling. Your new home."

I knew that it was new in more than one sense of the word, despite its eighteenth-century-style-clapboards, painted a dark green, and its multipaned windows. This was one of the houses that Guy's father built from time to time as investments. While we were still on that Caribbean island, the elder Nordeens had phoned to suggest that we occupy the house, even though it still lacked a few finishing touches. We had accepted promptly.

"It's lovely," I said, and it was, with its graceful proportions, its white shutters gleaming against the dark clapboards, its window boxes spilling scarlet petunias.

He stopped the car opposite the line of flagstones that led across the newly seeded lawn to the front porch. We had gotten out and were taking luggage from the trunk when the house door opened and Guy's parents came out to greet us. As I was kissed, first by Mrs. Nordeen and then by her husband, I reflected that it was obvious where Guy got his good looks. His mother was tall, with a clean-featured face framed by prematurely white hair. His father also was tall, with graying blond hair and a face that, only a few years back, must have been as handsome as his son's.

Mrs. Nordeen put her arm around my waist as we walked toward the porch. "As I told you over the phone the last time we talked, we've furnished the living room,

36

more or less, and the dining room, and one upstairs bed-room. And of course we brought you kitchen utensils and china and such. We realize you'll want to choose your own things eventually, but in the meantime maybe these will do."

"I'm sure they'll more than do."

"And I'm sure we're going to love each other." But of course she wasn't sure. In her blue eyes, so like Guy's, I read the mingled hope and apprehension any woman must feel when confronted with a daughter-in-law she has never met before.

"I'm sure also," I said.

In the living room, Guy's mother said, "These are all family pieces."

A Chinese Chippendale camelback sofa, upholstered in dark red. A Victorian love seat in a brocade of a lighter red. A pair of high-backed Victorian armchairs in sable brown velour. An obviously antique Kerman rug of muted red and ivory. "It's perfectly lovely, Mrs.—" I broke off.

"Call me Mother Nordeen. That is, if you want to."

"Thank you. Of course I want to."

She and I went upstairs to the bedroom, where Guy, now out in the garage with his father, had deposited the luggage. This room was equally attractive, with its old four-poster bed and chests of drawers of reddish mahog-any, its freshly painted pale green walls, and its starched lace curtains stirred by a sunset breeze.

My mother-in-law said, "I suppose you'll want to hire some help right away, at least a three-times-a-week cleaning woman."

"Oh, no! I'd rather try to get by on my own."

Even though Aunt Ellen always had employed domestic help for a few hours each week, I found after I moved into my loft that I had no knack with cleaning ladies and such. The ones that came my way talked on and on about their problems—ne'er-do-well husbands and rebellious kids—while I was trying to paint. I was, of course, expected to stop work and fix lunch for the both of us, even though I seldom even remembered to eat lunch when I was painting. They borrowed money from me and seldom paid it back. At last I decided that it would be easier, and much cheaper, to do my own housework.

"Well, if you change your mind, let me know, and I'll recommend someone."

She hesitated, and then went on, "One thing more. Guy called from Venice and told us he was following you to Florence in hope of persuading you to marry him. He also told us that you were the daughter of that Charity Edwards who died so tragically. I remember her, a very lovely young woman, and so very like you. I just wanted you to know that we already knew about it, and so it's entirely up to you whether you want to talk about it."

I smiled at her, liking her very much. "Thank you. Right now I'd rather—"

"Not talk about it? There's no need for you to talk about it ever, if you don't want to. Well, shall we go downstairs and join the men?"

We did. Then, with Mr. Nordeen in the lead, we descended to the still-unfinished paneled recreation room in the basement. Back in the living room, the four of us toasted the future with the carafe of sherry Mr. Nordeen had taken from a little rosewood liquor cabinet. Then Guy's mother said, "I took the liberty of making a pan of lasagna for your dinner. It's the only thing I can cook fairly well. You'll find it in the refrigerator."

"Oh, thank you!" I said. "And you'll share it, of course."

"Of course *not!* A newly married couple should dine alone their first night in their own home. We four will have plenty of dinners together in the future."

Two hours later, Guy and I faced each other across the round mahogany table in the dining room. We'd found not only lasagna in the refrigerator, but salad greens and tomatoes as well. Too, there was a bottle of champagne. Even though it seemed incongruously gala with lasagna, we were drinking it from the old-fashioned saucer champagne glasses I had found in the dining-room sideboard. ("I guess champagne flutes haven't caught on yet with Mother and Dad," Guy said.)

I took the last bite of the excellent lasagna on my plate and then laid down my fork. "Guy."

"Yes?"

"You've been Peggy Crofton's lover, haven't you?"

His eyes, very blue in the candlelight, looked startled and then amused. "What makes you ask that?"

"The way you two looked at each other."

"I had no idea it showed after all these years. But you're right. Peggy was my first—what shall I say? 'Girl' doesn't sound right. Maybe 'experience' will have to do."

"But she's so much older than you!"

"That's right. If it makes it any less shocking, it happened in Paris. She'd gone over there for clothes, or some damn thing. I was over there because my prep school grades had both astonished and delighted my parents. They'd decided to reward me with my first solitary trip abroad. I was seventeen."

"Seventeen! and she must have been—"

"Thirty-six, nineteen years older than I was. I remember her laughing about how she was more than twice my age. Don't look so shocked, Linda. I was damned lucky. Far better for a kid to have his first experience with someone like Peggy, rather than with a girl his own age who might have got pregnant, or a floozy who might have given him lord knows what."

Odd, I reflected, that his point of view should be so much more sophisticated than mine. After all, he was a small-towner, and I had been a Manhattanite. But while I'd been raised in modest comfort, he had grown up in affluence. While I was going to grammar school at P.S. 6 and vacationing at the Jersey shore, he was attending a fashionable prep school and spending his summers in Europe. Apparently all that made a difference.

"Don't be a prude, darling. Don't hold it against poor Peg. She didn't seduce me. It was the other way around. At least I like to think it was. And anyway, it was over long, long ago. She stayed on in Paris for almost a year, and when she finally came back I was eighteen, and interested in girls my own age. So try to be friends with Peggy."

He was smiling, but his voice had held an edge. I felt a moment's fear. Everything was so perfect. My beloved. This brand-new house. My nice parents-in-law. I mustn't let anything ruin it. Not Guy's account of a long-ago Paris summer. Not my memory of an even longer-ago August night in the woods. Not anything.

I said, "Sorry. I'm just a hick from Manhattan. But if you'll give me time, I'll catch onto your fancy small-town ways."

He laughed. "That's my girl."

When we'd finished dinner and cleared the table, there was still some champagne in the bottle. We carried it

40

into the living room, lit the fire Guy's parents had laid in the grate, and then, seated on the rug in front of the flames, polished off the champagne. One thing led to another, and we made love, with the firelight rosy on our naked bodies. Finally, carrying our clothes, we went upstairs and fell asleep in each other's arms in the big four-poster.

Sometime in the night I came abruptly awake. For a few seconds I was aware only of Guy's arm beneath my cheek, and his other arm slanting across my body, and the lacy pattern of starched curtains, evidently cast by a distant streetlight, on the wall. And then I began to feel it, a leaden depression.

Why had I not only consented but even insisted that we live in this town, when I'd grown up knowing intuitively it was the one place I should avoid?

And what made me think I could hold Guy's love? Why, tonight, our very first night in our own home, he had seemed on the verge of calling me a prig and a bore. The Peggy Croftons of the world were more his speed.

Then I began to wonder where it had come from, this sudden gloom. I had a sense of something in the air, something that had swirled up—from where? the basement? the first floor?—to thicken the air of this bedroom.

Maybe there was something wrong with this house.

My common sense reasserted itself then. Old houses might or might not sometimes be haunted, but not a house so new that you could almost smell the paint, and the not-yet-stained pine walls of the playroom in the basement.

My mood seemed to lighten a little. Naturally I was unsure of myself, I reflected. Naturally I worried about my relations with Guy's family and friends. And naturally

41

I was still affected by my childhood memories. But I would get over all that in time. I had to, because the negative aspects were as nothing compared to what life with Guy could hold for me in this town.

I felt calmer, but still wide awake. Afraid I might awaken Guy, I eased myself out of my husband's arms and onto the far side of the bed. When I finally fell asleep, birds were chirping. Robins, perhaps. Raised in the big city, I could not be sure.

THE GIVE of the mattress under someone's weight. The fragrance of shaving lotion.

I opened my eyes. Bright sunlight showed me Guy sitting on the edge of the bed, smiling down at me. He was a ready-for-business Guy I had never seen before, dressed in a dark blue pin-striped suit and blue shirt, set off by a navy blue tie with tiny red polka dots. But the clear skin, still tan from the Caribbean sun, was the same, and the intensely blue eyes, and the blond hair still damp from the shower.

"Well, wife, I'm off to the jute mill."

I sat up. "What time is it?"

"A little after eight."

"Oh, Guy! Why didn't you call me? I was going to fix you a lovely breakfast."

Days ago I'd planned his first back-to-the-office breakfast. I'd checked last night to be sure I had the ingredients, orange juice and eggs and bacon and muffins and strawberry jam. And I would have been up in time to fix it if it hadn't been for that absurd stretch of wakefulness the night before.

"No matter. Mom and Dad left a box of my favorite cereal in the kitchen." An automobile horn sounded outside. "There's Dad now."

43

"You're driving into Hartford with him?"

"We've always driven to the office together. Why don't you take the Mustang and do a little exploring today? See you tonight."

He kissed me and then left the bedroom. A few seconds later I heard Mr. Nordeen's car back out of the drive. I took a shower, dressed in a blue cotton caftan—it was another unseasonably warm day—and went down to the kitchen. Guy had left his cereal bowl and his cup, with a little coffee still in it, on the red-and-white checked cloth that covered the breakfast-nook table. So, after all, he was not the perfect husband. Rather pleased that he was not—a man skilled at domestic tasks has less need of someone to run his household—I carried his used dishes to the sink, rinsed them and put them in the drain rack. Then I fixed my orange juice and coffee and carried them to the breakfast nook.

For a while after Guy had awakened me in that sun-flooded bedroom, I had thought that my strange fit of depression had passed with the darkness. But now in this bright kitchen, so still that the refrigerator's hum sounded loud, I felt it creeping back—that foreboding, that sense of inadequacy, that conviction that in returning here I had launched myself into waters beyond my depth. I sipped my coffee, trying to lose my dark mood in thoughts of the many tasks that lay ahead of me. First, I would go over the whole house and make a tentative list of what additional furniture we needed . . .

The phone rang out in the lower hall.

I went out to the phone table and lifted the instrument from its cradle. "Hello."

"Mrs. Nordeen?" It was a masculine voice, pleasant and young-sounding.

I was still so unused to my new title that I almost said,

44

"No, this is her daughter-in-law," but I caught myself in time. "Yes, this is Mrs. Nordeen."

"I'm Jack Payson. I run the artist's supply shop here. The Art Stall, I call it." He paused. "I hear you're a painter."

"Well, I do book jackets."

"I think you'll find I have any supplies you might need. And whether you buy anything or not, I'd certainly like to have you drop in soon. It's exciting that Wessex now has a full-time artist. Lots of painters come here in the summertime, but after Labor Day they go back to SoHo or whatever. So please stop by."

That was what I needed, not moving about this too silent house with pen and a pad of paper in my hand. As soon as possible, I needed to meet people like this friendly sounding man. I needed to move around this pretty village until I was thoroughly acquainted with it. Surely that was the way to rid myself of this unease.

I said, "Where is your shop?"

"On Main Street, two doors north of the Wessex Savings Bank."

"I may be there this morning. I do need some brush cleaner and charcoal."

"Splendid! See you soon, Mrs. Nordeen."

About an hour later I drove the Mustang along the street bordering the river and then turned left onto Main. Again I marveled at the sophisticated attractiveness of the wares—fine luggage, antique furniture, beautiful flower arrangements—on display behind plate-glass windows. It was almost like a small-scale New England version of Palm Beach's Worth Avenue.

A name on a window caught my attention. Dilsey Wolsifer's Bakery. Dilsey, my grandmother's friend, whom the police had called to take care of me after my

45

mother's body had been found that long-ago morning.

So, just as Guy had said, she was still alive and still in business, although now she sold only baked goods.

On impulse, I turned into a vacant parking space. Before buying my charcoal and brush cleaner, I would call on Dilsey. I walked back to the bakery and went inside.

Two customers, both middle-aged women, stood peering down through the counter's glass top. Behind the counter stood a much older woman, tall and gaunt and with a vaguely familiar face framed in iron gray hair. The startled look that leaped into her gray eyes behind their rimless glasses told me that she knew who I was.

But she gave me no greeting. Instead, she said to one of the women, "I think you'd like that spice cake, Mrs. Warren. Mrs. Dunworthy told me yesterday that it's about the best spice cake she ever tasted. By the way, did you hear that the Dunworthys have bought a house in Spain?"

"No!" one of the customers said.

"In Málaga, I think it is." They went on talking about the Dunworthys while I stood awkwardly by, wondering why Dilsey was snubbing me. Dilsey, who'd spoken to me with such tender sorrow that terrible morning seventeen years before.

Each of the women bought a spice cake. Then, even though it was obvious that Dilsey wanted them to linger, they said good-bye and left. She turned to me reluctantly. "Yes?"

"Dilsey?" I had always called her that. Probably both she and my mother had felt that "Miss Wolsifer" was too big a mouthful for a small child to manage. "Don't you know me? I thought you did when I walked in. I'm Linda, Charity Edwards's daughter."

46

"How could I help recognizing you? You're the spitting image of your mother." After a moment she added, "But I couldn't believe it when I heard you'd married Guy Nordeen and were coming back here."

Chilled by the aloofness in her eyes, I asked, "Why couldn't you believe it?"

"Because in all these years you haven't come back here to visit—"

She broke off, but I knew what she had been about to say. I had never returned to Wessex to visit my mother's grave.

I had never wanted to visit that Presbyterian churchyard. I still did not want to, although I couldn't have said why. I'd do so sooner or later, of course, but it would be with reluctance.

Behind me the bell above the shop door tinkled. With obvious relief Dilsey turned to the new customer, a freckle-faced boy of about ten. I lingered for a moment, feeling chilled and bewildered, and then walked out. Someday I would challenge her as to the reason for her unfriendliness, but not today.

Out on the sidewalk, I turned to my right. I passed the Wessex Savings Bank. Next to it was a bookstore, and next to that the Art Stall.

The shop was empty, except for a man who stood with one foot braced on the floor and the other haunch resting on the counter. He held a white china mug in his hand. He placed the mug on the counter and walked toward me, a lean man with dark curly hair. His clothing—white duck trousers, white shirt partially unbuttoned to reveal matted dark hair on a sun-bronzed chest—suggested the tennis court rather than a business establishment.

"Mrs. Nordeen?"

Over the phone, a certain assurance in his voice had led me to think he was attractive. But I hadn't expected this sort of good looks, the sort one associates with men whose chief career is pleasing women. In Venice I'd seen quite a few men who looked like Jack Payson, handsome young Italians hanging around the expensive hotels and bars, obviously on the lookout for not-too-young women tourists with Vuitton handbags. . . .

"Yes, I'm Linda Nordeen."

"I'm Jack Payson." His thick-lashed brown eyes—bedroom eyes, my Aunt Ellen would have called them—smiled down at me. "Now let me bring you a cup of tea."

"No, thank you. I have several things to—"

"Let me assure you that nothing you have to do could be more important than making the acquaintance of this tea. A friend of mine brought it home last week from Singapore. It's not just tea. It's an experience. Lord! Sounds like an advertising slogan. Maybe I should be on Madison Avenue instead of running this shop."

Then, coaxingly: "Can't we spend a few minutes getting acquainted? As you can see, business is slow. I feel so damned bored when no one comes in."

I thought, why not? After all, I wanted to get to know the townspeople. Besides, after Dilsey's puzzling snub, his friendliness was comforting. "Thank you. I would like some tea."

He pointed to a chair near where he'd been perched on the counter. "Sit ye down. Sugar? Cream? Lemon?"

"Just one lump of sugar, please." I sat down.

He went out through a partly opened door at the rear of the shop. I heard him climbing stairs. So he must have living quarters up there. While I waited, I looked at the matted watercolors and unframed oils along one wall. One or two I liked, and several others seemed quite com-

48

petent, but others obviously were the work of amateurs with no talent whatsoever.

He came back bearing an exquisite cup and saucer of pale green bone china. I said, "What a lovely cup!"

"The last of the set. I use it only for special guests."

The tea really was very good, as fragrant as any jasmine tea I'd ever had, but more delicate.

Jack Payson said, "Might as well get the clichéd questions out of the way. How do you like our little town?"

"It's very attractive. Were you born here?"

"Oh, no. I was raised in Massachusetts. Several years ago I came down here to visit my cousin. You met her yesterday evening, by the way. Peggy Crofton."

Easy to believe they were cousins. They looked alike, although I judged him to be about fifteen years her junior.

"I liked the town, and I'd just inherited a little money, and so I opened this shop. I've been here ever since."

"Do you like running it?"

"In the summer it's fine. You see, I not only sell artists' supplies. I've got a little studio in back. I give art lessons."

Maybe my face already had betrayed my guess about what sort of man he was, because he grinned and said, "You'd be surprised how many women whose children are grown and whose husbands are—well, preoccupied, discover that they have artistic inclinations. I instruct them. Not that I'm much of a painter."

No, but you have other talents, probably quite profitable ones, I thought, noticing the gold watch banded around his lean brown wrist. Like the chains gleaming through the tendrils of dark hair on his chest, it had an expensively heavy look. "Were some of those pictures on the wall painted by your students?"

"How did you guess?"

I could imagine those women, flattered right down to their Ferragamo heels when he asked to hang their work in his shop.

He asked, "Had you ever seen Wessex before?"

"Yes, as a matter of fact I was born here, and lived here until I was six."

Might as well tell him that. He'd hear about it anyway, sooner or later. Maybe he'd already heard. Maybe, if she knew about it, his cousin Peggy Crofton had told him.

*Had* Peggy known about my mother's death? She must have, I realized. According to Guy, she had come here about twenty-five years ago, following her marriage to the richest man in town. That meant that she had been here several years by the time my mother was drowned.

Jack Payson asked, "How come you left our village at the tender age of six?"

"My mother died. Some relatives adopted me and took me to New York."

"Oh! Sorry. Say, wait a minute! I think I remember hearing something about a young widow with a small daughter, somebody named Edmonton or something like that—"

"Edwards. My mother's name was Charity Craig Edwards." Saying her name brought her memory so vividly close that my heart twisted.

"Do you remember the house where you lived?"

"Some things about it."

"I've seen it. In fact, it was after I described it to someone that I heard about—about your mother's death. It's a beautiful old house in a beautiful spot in the woods. Built in the late seventeen-hundreds, I'd say."

"I wouldn't know. I just know that my mother inherited it from my grandmother."

50

"Does the property belong to you?"

"No. My adoptive parents sold the property for me and put the money in trust until my eighteenth birthday." That money had paid for my expenses at Barnard, and later on for the furnishings of my SoHo loft. "I have no idea who owns the house now."

Jack Payson said, "It looks like a place that's passed through a number of hands and has ended up with someone who doesn't give a damn about it. The River Realty down the street might be able to tell you who owns it. They've handled most of the real estate transactions around here since the year one."

"Maybe I'll ask. I noticed their office as I drove up Main Street."

I knew I would ask. Suddenly I needed very much to see that house. I placed my empty teacup and its saucer on the counter. "Now, as I said over the phone, I need some charcoal—"

"Oh, please! Don't rush off."

"I must. I have a lot of things to do." And button up your shirt, I wanted to add. Don't waste all that virility on me.

I went out a few minutes later, carrying a paper bag that contained a stick of charcoal and a bottle of brush cleaner, and turned to my left. The real estate office was only a few doors away. An arc of gold-leaf letters on the window said, "River Realty." Smaller letters below said, "George Orme, Licensed Realtor."

I went in. A girl of about eighteen sat typing at a small desk. "Help you?"

Her green dress was of some sort of synthetic material, her nails were bitten, and her hair looked as if she had given herself an inexpert home permanent. It was rather nice, I reflected, to realize that not all Wessex residents looked as if they had stepped out of the pages of *Country Life*.

"I wanted to inquire about an old house—"

"Mr. Orme isn't in right now. He's out with a client." She nodded toward the other desk, a larger one, near the rear wall. "But if you wait, he'll be glad to show you the place."

"That won't be necessary. I just wanted to get some information about it. Maybe you could help me."

She looked dubious. "I'll try. Have a seat."

I sat down in a straight chair beside her desk. She asked, "Where is the house?"

"I'm not sure." I had a feeling that it had been somewhere to the north of the village limits, but I wasn't at all certain. "All I'm sure of is that a woman named Charity Edwards owned it up until about seventeen years ago."

"I'll see if that name's in our files."

She went to a line of wooden filing cabinets against one wall, pulled out a narrow drawer, and leafed through cards. "Here it is. Charity Craig Edwards. We've got the house cross-filed."

She moved to another cabinet, leafed through a drawer. "Here it is. Property inherited by Linda Edwards, a minor. Her guardians listed it with us, and we sold it to Arnold Crukshank. Why, I remember him! He was some kind of a poet and he looked like Longfellow. Long gray beard and everything. He would come to the grammar school twice a year and read his poems to us kids." She turned to look at me. "I couldn't understand much of it, but it sounded nice. He died when I was eight or nine."

"And after that?"

"What do you mean, after that? He died, that's all. Oh, you mean the house." She turned back to the file. "Harold Framm bought it. Didn't live in it or rent it. He buys properties on speculation. He sold it to a Charles Boyd—I don't even know him!—and after almost two years he sold it to Joseph and Caroline Pell. I do know them. Nice, sort of elderly. Maybe they meant to fix it up, either to live in it or resell it, but instead they went to Florida, oh, maybe four years ago and haven't been back, although they still pay taxes on the place."

And so only one person, an old poet, had lived there since my mother and I had. And ever since his death the house had stood empty. "Can you tell me how to reach the place?"

"Sure. Go out past the lake for about half a mile. You'll see a dirt road leading off to the right. There are a few houses along that road, mainly rental cottages that are closed now. They're all close to the highway. Keep going for about two miles. The road ends in a turnaround in front of the property you asked about."

"Thank you very much." I stood up.

"Hey! Aren't you going to leave your name?"

"Not right now. If I find I'm interested in the place, I'll be back. Thank you again."

A few minutes later I was passing the small lake on the town's outskirts. Perhaps the squawking Canadian geese had continued their journey north. Anyway, today there were only the haughty swans, floating above their mirrored images. I found the dirt road, turned up it. The summer cottages the girl had mentioned were modest indeed, one-story frame structures with cylinders of bottled gas outside their kitchen windows. I was sure, though, that during the season they rented for a pretty sum.

53

No more cottages now, just mingled pines and broad-leafed trees bordering the road. I rounded a curve. Ahead was the turnaround and, just beyond it, the house, set back in a weed-grown yard surrounded by a split-rail fence with several of its rails missing. In my memory that fence had been painted white. Time had bleached it to a uniform gray.

Heart beating fast, I left the car. There was only a gap where the gate had been. And, of course, no flowers bordered the walk, that walk whose bricks had felt rough to my small bare feet that August night long ago. Many of the bricks were missing. The house's brown shingles, at least here on the south-facing facade, were sun-bleached and split and curling. All the windows were boarded up.

I went around to the side of the house. If I remembered correctly, those smaller windows, set high in the wall, were the kitchen's. Yes, just below the boarded-up windows was the rack, half fallen down now, on which the bottled gas had rested.

A few feet away were the boarded-up windows of Sara Breed's room.

I stood there in the knee-high weeds, vaguely conscious of a bee humming in the summerlike air, and thought of myself crossing the kitchen, its stove and sink and shiny refrigerator looking unfamiliar in the moonlight. I'd looked into Sara's empty room and called her name, even though I had remembered that Wednesday was one of her nights off.

Where had she been at that moment? Pedaling her bike toward her aunt's house on the other side of town? Or still down at the pool with the all-but-unconscious woman who had been my mother?

I crossed my arms in front of me, hands grasping my shoulders. I wished I hadn't come here. But no. I'd have been drawn here sooner or later. Better to get it over with, and then try to get on with my life as Mrs. Guy Nordeen.

And that pool. Best to go look at it, right now. Best to get that over with, too.

I went back to the road and walked down it perhaps fifty yards. Just as I remembered it, here was the entrance to a path, although I'd feared it might be overgrown after all these years. Perhaps deer and raccoons and other wild animals used it. I emerged beside the stream and followed its noisy course for a few yards until I reached the little falls. Below the falls was the pool, wider and of course much stiller than the stream that fed it. The footbridge still spanned it. I descended the abruptly sloping path and walked out onto the bridge.

I looked at the bank and thought of Sara Breed, one thick arm around my mother's slender waist as she half coaxed, half dragged the drugged woman into the water—

No! It couldn't have happened like that. No matter what Sara had confessed, it couldn't have. There had to be more to it than had come out at the trial. Sara loved my mother, loved me. I remembered her round, coarse face, beaming with gratification and pride as she carried the cake she had baked for my sixth birthday into the dining room.

True, according to that jury she had gone insane. But even insanity has its logic. Insane people can and do give *reasons* for their acts, no matter how grotesque those reasons may seem to others. Sara had given no reason. "I don't know," she had said, when asked why she had drugged my mother's food, why she had brought her to this pool. . . .

Would Sara tell me why she had done it? It seemed unlikely that I could succeed where a judge and lawyers and psychiatrists had failed. And yet as I stood there in the late-morning sunlight I had a feeling that, for some reason I could not put my finger on, Sara might tell me the truth.

Was she still alive? More than likely. According to those newspaper clippings Aunt Ellen had saved, Sara had been only thirty-two at the time of her trial.

Was she still at that hospital for the criminally insane in—What was the name of the town. Claverly? Yes, that was it.

Of course, if her aunt was still alive, I could ask her where and how Sara was now. But I shrank from the idea. How that woman must have suffered, first because of her orphaned niece's retardation, and then because of that senseless crime.

Best just to go to the hospital. And best not to phone first. They might put me off for one reason or another. But if I just turned up there and made my request with sufficient urgency. . . .

Where was Claverly? I had an impression that it was quite near.

The map. There was a Connecticut road map in the Mustang's glove compartment. I left the bridge, climbed the path through the warm silence. Back in the car I unfolded the map. Yes, here was Claverly, about a dozen miles to the north, just off the interstate highway.

I really didn't want to go to that grim place, I realized, didn't want to face the woman who, for whatever reason, had murdered my mother. But now that the idea had come to me, I had to follow it through. Otherwise, the thought of Sara Breed, only a few miles away, would continue to haunt me, just when I needed all my energy to make a place for myself in this town, my husband's town.

I restored the map to the glove compartment. I took one last look at the house, falling to ruin in its weedy yard. Then I turned the car and drove down the dirt road.

## SEVEN

A LITTLE MORE than an hour later, I followed a white-uniformed nurse down a short hall. She opened a door and then said to me, "Miss Breed is in there. Please go on in. I'll be back in twenty minutes."

It had taken me quite a while to get this far. At the reception desk I'd been told that the previous day had been visiting day, and that I had best return the next week. When I'd insisted that I needed to see the patient right then, the receiving nurse had directed me to an office down the hall. There, a pleasant-faced red-haired woman—Carol Hernshaw, R.N., the nameplate on her desk said—had taken my name and then asked me, "Are you a relative of Miss Breed's?"

"No."

"Then why—"

"It was because she—she killed my mother that she was shut up here."

The woman said, in an appalled voice, "Oh, my dear!" then, after a moment: "But even so, why do you feel you must see her immediately?"

Since there seemed to be no help for it, I told her. My marriage, and my subsequent return to a town I'd never expected to see again. My anxiety to fit into the community the way my husband wanted me to. And my sense that I simply could not until after I had faced what had happened to my mother when I was a young child and had tried my best to understand it.

She tapped a pencil on her desk. "I think I understand," she said finally. "I'll have her brought to the small visiting room." She lifted the phone, spoke briefly. Then she said, "But please don't get your hopes up. In all her years here, no one has been able to get her to explain why she acted as she did. And even if she does give you some sort of reason, you can scarcely take it as gospel. She's been diagnosed as schizophrenic, you know."

"I realize I mustn't put too much faith in anything she might tell me. But I really would appreciate seeing her."

She pushed a button. "I'll have someone show you the way."

Now I stepped into the visiting room. The door closed behind me. I gained an impression of cheery yellow walls, framed landscapes, and green-and-yellow plaid draperies, which almost, but not quite, canceled out the effect of the barred windows.

Sara Breed sat in a tub chair upholstered in the same plaid that hung at the windows. I would have recognized her anywhere, I felt. Her short hair was entirely gray now, but it still had the spiky look I remembered. And her round face had aged scarcely at all.

Her jaw dropped. Her hazel eyes stared at me for a moment more before she cried, "Oh, missus, you've come back!" She clasped her hands together. "Oh, missus! You wasn't hurt after all."

After a moment I said, "Hello, Sara."

"But you cut your hair! Why'd you do that, missus? You had such pretty hair."

"Maybe I shouldn't have cut it." I drew a straight chair close to her and sat down. Here was a break I hadn't anticipated. She thought I was my mother. Therefore she might be more inclined to talk to me. Better make the most of it.

She said, "Where's Linda?"

"I didn't bring her with me. She's at home."

She frowned, the beginning of doubt in her eyes. "You really are all right, missus?"

I said swiftly, "Of course."

"How is it you're all right, after I—"

"I just am, that's all. Sara, why did you try to—hurt me?"

After a moment she leaned closer. "Lots of people asked me that, not just in this place, but before. I didn't tell them anything. The voices said I must never tell anybody. But I'll tell *you*."

"What voices?"

"The ones that told me what to do. They told me I'd find a little bag on my closet shelf. And I did find it."

"What was in it?"

"Powder, white powder. The voices said I was to sprinkle some in your soup, and your salad, and some in your dessert—spiced applesauce it was that night—and some in your Sanka."

I said, feeling cold all over, "And then?"

"They said I was to wait until you'd been in bed a while. Then I was to get you up and take you down to the pool—" Suddenly she whimpered. "You're sure I didn't hurt you bad?"

"It's all right, Sara."

"I never wanted to hurt you, and I tried not to, even when I was holding you under in that—" She broke off and then said, "But I had to do it. The voices said I had to."

60

"Where did the voices come from?"

"My head. They were inside my head. Do you think it was all a dream, missus? I mean, my taking you down to the pool—"

"No, it wasn't a dream."

"I guess not. They wouldn't have brought me here just because I had a dream. You want me to come back to work for you?"

"Not right now, Sara. Don't you like it here?"

"Oh, yes. It's nice. We watch TV and go for walks and make things. You'll come to see me again, missus?"

"Yes, Sara, although I'm not sure just when."

"You come soon. And bring Linda next time."

A door in the far wall opened, and a woman in a pink nurse's-aide uniform came in. "Time for you to go back with the others, Sara." Then, to me: "Miss Hernshaw wants you to stop by her office if you don't mind."

Sara stood up docilely. As the nurse's aide was leading her out, she looked back at me and said, "Now you'll come back soon, won't you?"

"Yes, Sara."

A few moments later, in Miss Hernshaw's office, I said, "She talked, but it didn't make any sense. You see, she thought I was my mother."

"You didn't contradict that?"

"No, I was afraid that she might not go on talking if I told her she was wrong."

"What did she tell you?"

"That voices, voices in her head, told her to do what she did to my mother."

Miss Hernshaw nodded. "Typical of schizophrenics. Well, I'll make up a report for her doctor."

"She says that she's quite happy here."

"I'm glad. Everyone here likes her. It's strange how some schizophrenics can have one violent, even murderous, episode, and after that remain completely gentle and agreeable."

I thanked her again and said good-bye.

As I drove back along the highway toward Wessex, I reflected that at least I'd learned a little from my visit to Sara. She was definitely insane. Her talk of "voices" proved that. And so almost certainly my mother had met death at her hands, hard as that had been for me to believe. But the source of the barbiturates was more puzzling than ever. I might have been able to believe that she'd found a bottle of sleeping pills beside the road, say. But her story of finding a little bag of white powder on her closet shelf, just where the voices had told her to look—that made no sense whatsoever.

True, someone could have gotten in. As I remembered, the doors of that house were never locked. But why would anyone—

A sign caught my eye. Pete's Pizza. I stopped, had a belated lunch, and then drove on through the afternoon sunlight.

I N WESSEX, I stopped off at the supermarket. Thus I didn't reach the house until around four o'clock. A blue panel truck stood out front. WESSEX INTERIORS, the sign on its side said, and in smaller letters below: Paper hanging, wall paneling, floor finishing. I had just parked the Mustang in the driveway and taken a bag of groceries from the back seat when two men in white coveralls came around the corner of the house. Both carried tool kits.

The shorter and older of the men said, "Mrs. Nordeen?"

"Yes."

"We've oiled the panels in the playroom and put a first coat of varnish on the floor. Best not to step on it for at least twenty-four hours. We'll be back next week to put on the second coat."

"Thank you."

I went into the house and carried my groceries back to the kitchen. Even though the door to the basement stairs was closed, I could smell varnish and something else, probably the oil the workmen had put on the walls. I moved briskly about, assembling the ingredients and utensils I would need for the making of my own version of chicken pot pie, a recipe based not on leftovers but on

chicken breasts freshly poached in broth. None of those
witticisms about the bride's cooking could be applied to
me. At my own request, Aunt Ellen had begun to teach
me to cook when I was ten. I had always found turning
out an excellent meal one of life's dependable pleasures.

Tonight I especially enjoyed the prospect of cooking.
At the inn where we had spent our Caribbean honeymoon, all meals had been provided. Therefore this would
be the first dinner I had ever prepared for Guy.

Gradually, though, my mood of pleasant anticipation
began to slip away. Perhaps thoughts of that decaying old
house and of that incongruously cheerful hospital visiting
room kept getting in the way of my usual pleasure in
measuring, sifting, and testing broth-simmered vegetables with a fork. For whatever reason, I began to feel a
dull depression as I moved between countertop and
stove.

There's something wrong with this house.

As before, the thought had seemed to leap of its own
accord into my mind. And as before, I recognized it as
absurd. What could be "wrong" with the atmosphere of a
house so new that men were still working on it? A house
in which no one had even been born, let alone died?

No, what was weighting my spirit was the day I had
spent. Perhaps it had been necessary to go to that house
and hospital. In fact, I was still sure it had been a first
step toward adjusting to my life here in Wessex. But it
had been depressing, too.

Better not to tell Guy about going to the house, or
about visiting Sara Breed. I felt he might disapprove. And
I didn't want anything to mar our evening together.

When Guy came home at almost six, he looked as I had
never seen him until then, tired and out of sorts. Over our

pre-dinner drinks in the living room, scotch and water for him and sherry for me, he told me that his first day back at the office had been a rough one. A telephone call to a valued customer in Chicago had brought him the bad news that sometime while Guy was in Europe and the Caribbean, the Chicagoan had decided to switch to another importing firm. For a moment I had the feeling that, at least subconsciously, he blamed me for the loss of that important customer. Then I realized how fantastic that notion was. He was tired, that was all.

At the dinner table, set with Nordeen crystal candlesticks and white china, and with the sterling flatware Aunt Ellen and Uncle Brad had given us in New York, Guy was just as appreciative of the food as I had hoped he would be. Then, halfway through the meal, he asked, "What did you do today?"

"Mostly I just drove around."

I felt a twinge of guilt. But now that I had seen that he was weary and worried, I was more than ever convinced that I must not tell him how I really had spent the day.

"Oh! And I went to the Art Stall for some charcoal and brush cleaner."

"Jack Payson's place?"

"Yes. He was very cordial. He phoned this morning and suggested I visit his shop, and when I got there he insisted that I have a cup of tea."

"I'll bet he was cordial!"

I frowned. "What do you mean?"

"That guy's the randiest tomcat in town. Don't get friendly with him. If you have to go to his shop, be sure everything is strictly business. Better yet, don't go there at all. If you need paints or anything, I can pick them up in Hartford."

"Oh, Guy! Surely you don't think I'd be susceptible to someone as obvious as he is!"

"No, but people might think you are. Everyone in town knows his reputation."

"You mean that he's a no-no where the best people are concerned? How can that be? If he's Peggy Crofton's cousin, and if Peggy runs this town—"

I broke off. Those blue eyes had narrowed. He said, "Just take my word for it and stay away from him. Peggy is an entirely different matter. He can harm your standing here, she can help it."

He gave a forced-looking smile. "And don't go sprouting claws, Linda. On you they don't look good."

We ate in silence for a while. Then he asked a question about the playroom walls, and I answered. But the mood I'd hoped for had been shattered, and not even the lemon mousse I'd prepared for dessert could restore it.

We did not make love that night. Right after the ten o'clock news, Guy went up to bed. I spent perhaps half an hour at not really necessary tasks, plumping up sofa cushions and rearranging magazines Mrs. Nordeen had placed on the coffee table. Then I went upstairs. When I slipped into bed Guy was asleep, or pretending to be.

OUR ESTRANGEMENT did not last, of course. The next night we went to Guy's parents' house, one of the handsome late eighteenth-century houses on Main Street, for an excellent dinner prepared by their cook, a Finnish woman who had been with them since before Guy was born. Then we went home and made love and fell asleep in each other's arms.

The next day, a Saturday, we packed a lunch and started out for a picnic spot that, Guy said, not many people knew about. We drove out of town a few miles and then turned onto a series of county roads. Finally Guy piloted the Mustang down a steep dirt turnoff to a swift stream running along a valley. We crossed an ancient-looking iron bridge. Beyond it, at the foot of a narrow road that led a winding course up the valley's opposite slope, a wooden sign warned in red letters, DANGER! NO THOROUGHFARE.

"Don't worry," Guy said. "We'll stop before we get to the dangerous part."

In second gear we drove up the narrow, deeply rutted road. The hillside had been cut away in places to provide space for turning a vehicle around. Finally we stopped in one such widened space. To show me the reason for the sign back at the bridge, Guy took me on foot around the next bend. From the road's outer edge the earth fell steeply away, studded with cedars. And the road itself had been so narrowed by erosion that even an expert driver might easily go over.

I said, "I should think they would have put up a barrier to keep people from driving up here."

"They have, several times. But deer hunters and such keep taking the barriers down."

We went back to the car, took out our picnic basket and climbed up above the road to where we had a view of rolling hills and a distant lake. Once we'd eaten our fill of ham sandwiches and fruit and cookies, we stretched out and turned our faces up to that marvelously warm October sun.

A lovely day. But now I knew that there could be stormy weather in Paradise. And so the next day I was not too surprised, just depressed, when at the breakfast table we fell to arguing, almost quarreling, over an editorial in the Hartford Sunday newspaper. The fact that a couple of days later I couldn't even recall the subject of the editorial made our argument over it all the more dismaying.

What was wrong? All those weeks in the Caribbean we had not had one disagreement. Why did we seem to get on each other's nerves now? I knew he loved me, and I certainly loved him. And yet, sometimes, that wonderful moment in Florence when he'd found me at the straw market seemed not just weeks ago but ages.

The last day of October, that unseasonably perfect weather broke. Temperatures plummeted. By the middle of the month, winds and freezing rain had whipped the last of the scarlet and yellow leaves from the trees. Trying to ignore both the weather and the puzzled unease in my heart, I kept busy. I furnished the two other bedrooms, partly with pieces from the village's antique shops, partly with reproductions from a Hartford furniture store, and partly with contemporary objets d'art—Italian mirrors and Irish crystal vases and English prints—from Nordeen Importers. I spent hours each day vacuuming and dusting and polishing, although at my mother-in-law's continued urging I did employ a cleaning woman twice a week.

And I tried to paint, in a room over the garage that I had turned into a studio. During our few days in New York after our return from the Caribbean, I had arranged with a publisher to do the cover for a forthcoming children's book. In late November the manuscript arrived, a charming story about a pair of seals who, rashly, adopted an infant walrus who already outweighed the two of them together. Eagerly I set to work on the cover painting.

But it was no good. The seals and their enormous adopted child seemed to just sit there on the paper, with none of the spirit and charm the writer had given them. Finally, in despair, I called up the publisher and said I was sending the manuscript back. My failure to even finish the painting disturbed me deeply. In the past, no matter how badly an assignment was going, I never had just abandoned it.

The next day the weather looked threatening, with clouds boiling up in the northwest. Nevertheless, as soon as Guy and his father had driven off to work, I changed to jogging clothes. In New York I had been one of the runners weaving their way among the pedestrians along SoHo sidewalks. Lately I had taken up running again, in the hope that regular and strenuous exercise would help my malaise of spirit.

69

I ran down the driveway, turned to my right, then right again along the road that paralleled the river. I passed an attractive wooden sign that, with letters painted in gothic script, invited visitors to attend the village's four churches: Catholic, Episcopalian, Congregational, and Presbyterian. Suddenly I wondered why I still had not visited my mother's grave in the Presbyterian churchyard. Was it some kind of subconscious denial of the reality of her death? Was that why I was avoiding the sight of a stone with her name on it? Or was there something else that held me back from visiting that churchyard?

Lost in my thoughts, I ran on, only vaguely aware of an occasional mutter of thunder. After more than a mile, I turned to my right up a graveled road, newly built by a subdivider. Trees walled both sides of the road, some with trunks encircled by a strip of red cloth. Those would be saved when the rest were slaughtered to make room for houses.

A flash of lightning, making the dark day brilliant for an instant. Almost immediately afterward, an ear-splitting thunderclap. A few large drops of cold rain spattering on my head and shoulders. And then the deluge.

I turned around, into the teeth of the storm. Rain slanted into my face with such force that I found it hard to breathe. I lowered my head and slogged on, miserably aware that, with home at least two miles away, my rain-soaked velour shirt and pants already weighed considerably more than when I had put them on.

Headlights illuminating the road ahead of me. A car stopping, a door opening. Aware only that I had been rescued, I got inside, closed the door.

It wasn't until then that I realized what car I had gotten into. It was the sleek Bentley that Jack Payson, with his taste for the more expensive things in life, had managed to acquire. I'd often seen him driving around town in it.

He said, "Hello, Aphrodite. You couldn't look any wetter if you'd just risen from the sea."

The streaming windshield cast a wavering gray light on his face. Could that be what suddenly made him look— odd? Oh, he was as handsome as ever with his satyrlike dark curls, and his heavy-lidded dark eyes and sensual mouth, but for an instant I had a sense that his features were becoming fluid and might reform themselves into quite a different face. . . .

He said, "I've got a raincoat on the back seat and a heavy turtleneck sweater in the trunk. What say we drive off into the trees and strip those wet clothes off you—"

I swung the door back and started to get out. "Hey! I'm only kidding." He reached across me, swung the door closed. I saw now that his face was no longer strange, just impish and amused. So it had been nothing but a trick of the watery gray light. He turned the ignition key. "See? I'm taking you straight home. But don't you think you'd be warmer with my raincoat around you?"

He reached into the back seat. I leaned forward and he draped the coat around me. "Thank you," I said.

"Think nothing of it." He drove in silence for a while and then asked, "How's the work coming?"

"If you mean my painting, it isn't." I told him about my failure with the seals and their walrus orphan.

"Too bad. Maybe you'd work better in another setting. Why not try my studio? I told you I had one, didn't I?"

"Yes. It's where you give lessons to the summer ladies. Thanks, but I'll struggle along in my own studio."

71

"If you change your mind, the offer still stands. What else have you been doing with your time? Have you joined Peggy's Watch and Ward Society?"

"If you mean the Ladies' Village Society, I haven't joined yet. But she sent me an invitation to the fall meeting day after tomorrow. I'm going to it." I had better, I reflected unhappily. Guy might be very annoyed if I did not.

Jack turned into our driveway, stopped the car. "Here you are," he said, "safe and sound." He put his hand on my knee. "Come up and see me at the Art Stall sometime, anytime."

I said, "I believe this is yours," and lifted his hand and placed it on his own knee.

He laughed. "See you around, Linda."

"Sure. Thanks for the lift."

Leaving the raincoat beside him on the seat, I got out and ran through the downpour to the front door.

Peggy crofton's house, set far back from Main Street, was the largest in Wessex. A rosy brick Colonial with white pillars, it looked like a larger version of Jefferson's Monticello.

The afternoon of the meeting, the graveled circular drive was lined with cars. I left the Mustang and walked through cold sunlight to the wide veranda. A brown-skinned man of sixty-odd, in dark trousers and a white jacket, answered the doorbell. Several inches shorter than me and very thin, he looked like an overaged jockey. Scarcely the sort of impressive butler who must once have guarded this magnificent doorway. But then, these days it was hard for even the very rich to obtain the sort of servants you see in those thirties movies.

He told me in a Jamaican accent that I would find the ladies upstairs in the ballroom. At the top of a flight of sweeping stairs I turned to my right and walked along a broad hallway. Easy to know where the ballroom was. Even climbing the stairs I had heard feminine voices, dozens of them. I went through a wide doorway. On the other side of the huge room, about fifty women sat on gilt chairs facing a broad desk. Peggy Crofton sat behind the desk with a red-haired woman, probably the recording secretary, beside her. Peggy waved to me and mouthed the words, "Sit down, please."

I did. The stout woman on the next chair gave me a friendly smile and introduced herself. "My husband was one of the plumbers who worked on that new house where you live." Well, it was nice to know that all sorts of women belonged to the Ladies' Village Society, not just the rich and fashionable.

Peggy rapped for order. The chatter died away. "First of all," Peggy said, "I want to introduce two newcomers. The first is Mrs. Guy Nordeen. Linda, will you stand up, please?"

I did, briefly, to a polite patter of applause.

"The second is my niece from San Francisco, Nicole Sorenson, who will be staying with me for several months. Many of you know her because she often before has spent several months here, but not all of you have met her. Stand up, Nicole."

She was a very pretty girl indeed, a slender brunette with large dark eyes and flashing dimples. And she was young, nineteen at the most.

When the girl had sat down, the members listened to, and approved, the minutes of the previous meeting. After that I learned that Guy hadn't been joking when he said that Peggy Crofton "ran" Wessex.

"I think our first order of business," she said, "should be the souvenir shop that the Carson Novelty Company wants to open here. I've seen their shops in other places. They look like something on the worst stretches of the Atlantic City boardwalk. I suggest that we tell Mr. Lindstrom—he's the prospective landlord—that if he rents to these people, we will not patronize the tenants of his other business properties. Will someone put that in the form of a motion?"

74

Someone did. Motion passed.

"Next there's the matter of the new sign Murray's Liquor Store wants to put on its roof. A big one, and neon at that! Will someone move that we appoint a committee to wait upon Mr. Murray and show him the error of his ways?"

Motion passed, committee appointed.

After that the chairman of the Beautification Committee, a thin, nervous-looking woman with thick-lensed glasses, reported that her committee wanted to plant red geraniums next spring instead of the usual pink petunias in the ornamental curbside urns in the business district. Spirited discussion followed. Someone said that many people disliked geraniums. Someone else said that petunias were "nothing-flowers, so terribly *limp.*" Somewhat to my surprise, Peggy did not join the discussion, but merely suggested, after about ten minutes, that it was time to vote. The geraniums won.

Peggy said, "Now I'm going to ask for a motion to adjourn, but first I'm going to ask our new member—at least we hope she'll be a new member," she went on, smiling at me, "to come up to the desk after the meeting and fill out a membership application."

I did so. As Peggy and I chatted—something about the coming Old House Tour, as I recall—I suddenly thought of thirty-six-year-old Peggy and seventeen-year-old Guy in that Parisian bedroom about a dozen years ago.

I went down to the driveway, got in my car, started home.

I was about halfway there when I was struck by the feeling that I had left my gold pen on the desk after I had made out my membership application. That pen was precious to me. Guy had bought it for me in Florence, while we were waiting for the American consul to obtain

75

our marriage license for us. I stopped at the curb and looked in my handbag. No pen. I made a U-turn at the next corner and went back to Peggy's house.

Still a few cars in the driveway. I got out and climbed the steps to the veranda, where the skinny little Jamaican, now wearing an alpaca jacket, was running a feather duster over a white wrought-iron settee. "Some of the ladies is still here," he said, and opened the door for me.

No sound of voices from the second floor. In fact, no sound at all. I climbed the stairs, walked back along the hall. In the ballroom, no one occupied the gilt chairs or sat behind the desk. But there were women here, all right. Evidently some kind of rump meeting was in progress, for I could hear a murmur of voices, coming from behind a slightly open door on the other side of the big room.

I walked to the desk. No pen. Could Peggy or someone have picked it up? I crossed to that almost closed door, knocked briefly, opened the door farther. "Excuse me, but—"

My voice died in my throat. Startled faces swung toward me. Peggy's, Nicole's, the recording secretary's, about a half-dozen others. They sat around a table in a small room, perhaps originally some sort of cloakroom or pantry. It might have been the wavering cigarette smoke in the room, but suddenly Peggy's face looked strange. It would be hard to say how. Not older. Perhaps ageless would be the word. Ageless and hard and baleful, like some primitive carving—

The moment passed. Nothing was strange. They were just a group of women—the sort of "in-group" you find in any fairly large organization—who had lingered to rehash the meeting and, perhaps, to trade a little gossip.

"Why, Linda!" Peggy said. The face between its twin

fans of hair was the same as always, poised and fine-featured and beautifully cared for. "What is it?"

"My gold pen. I think I left it here."

"So you did." Her chair scraped over the floor. "I put it away for you."

We walked together to the desk in the ballroom. She opened a drawer and handed me my pen.

"Oh, thank you!"

"Not at all. Now that you're back here, why not stay a while? We're going down to the library in a few minutes and have some tea or sherry or whatever."

"Oh, no, thank you. I must start thinking about dinner."

Out in the driveway I started my car and drove around the semicircle to the road. I felt frightened. What was happening to me? Thinking the other morning that some sort of transformation was taking place in Jack Payson's handsome face, and then this afternoon . . .

The chill word "hallucinations" came into my thoughts.

Even before today I had been behaving strangely. What sort of woman found herself unable, for any reason whatsoever, to visit her mother's grave?

I would visit it, right now.

Two or three minutes later I turned onto a quiet, up-ward-sloping street of medium-sized houses. The Presbyterian Church, built of pale tan stone, stood at the top of the street. Its churchyard lay between the building and a stand of deciduous trees, bare except for a few leathery-looking leaves that still clung to the oaks. I went into the churchyard and found my mother's grave almost immediately. Her headstone was a small slab of marble. There was no inscription, just her name, Charity Craig Edwards, and the dates of her birth and death.

As I stood there beside the rounded mound, she seemed very close to me, my lovely and gentle mother, closer than she had ever seemed in all the years since her death. Why had I been afraid to come here? Because that was what I had been, afraid. Now I would come here often, bringing evergreen branches for the next few weeks and, in the spring, azaleas and daffodils and iris—wild iris, if I could find them, because I had just remembered the pleasure I had once seen in her face when she came back from the woods, carrying a bouquet of the small, purple-blue flowers.

It was easing, that tension I had felt ever since I returned to Wessex. I wept for a moment, but quietly, feeling the silent tears slide down my cheeks.

Behind me I heard the church's heavy-sounding door open and close. I dried my tears with a handkerchief and then turned around. A white-haired man in a clerical collar stood on the wide brick walk that led to the church door. Plainly he had been watching me. I moved along one of the graveled paths toward him.

"Forgive me," he said, "but aren't you the new Mrs. Nordeen?"

I nodded. Perhaps by this time there wasn't a soul in Wessex who didn't know that I was the bride young Guy Nordeen had brought home.

"I'm Dr. Dorrance, the pastor of this church. I couldn't help noticing that you were visiting your mother's grave."

He was a gentleman. No hint in his gray eyes and clean-shaven face that he wondered why it had taken me so long to come here. "Yes," I said.

"Did you find your grandmother's grave also?"

My mother's mother. Like my father, she had died when I was not yet three. I had only one brief memory of her, helping me to rebuild a stack of wooden blocks that had collapsed.

"No," I said. "Where is her grave?"

"If you'll permit me, I'll show you."

We walked to an obviously older part of the cemetery, where a few marble angels and granite tombs stood among plainer memorials. My grandmother's was the plain kind, just a granite headstone giving her name, Martha Tolan Craig, and the place and date of her death. She had been born in Humility, Massachusetts, in 1897, and had died in 1966.

As I stood there, trying—and failing—to remember more about her than the smile on her face while she helped me rebuild my tower, Dr. Dorrance said, "Your great-grandmother is buried here too, you know."

I hadn't known. I was realizing now how little family history I knew, thanks to the fact that Uncle Brad and Aunt Ellen always had avoided talking to me about my mother or anything connected with her.

"Would you like for me to show you her grave?"

"Thank you very much."

As we moved deeper into the churchyard, he said, "Do you realize that you have only female ancestors buried here? I know from parish records that your great-grandmother was already a widow when she came here from Massachusetts. And I know that your father was buried in the Edwards family plot somewhere in New Jersey. I know because I had just been named assistant curate here at the time he died in that plane crash. But I don't know about your grandfather—your mother's father, I mean."

I searched my memory. "I know," I finally said. "He was in the navy during the Second World War. He was killed in battle in the South Pacific and buried at sea." I didn't know whether I had learned that from my grandmother, or my mother, or from overheard conversation between the Cartwrights. I just knew that I knew it.

"So that's it. Well, here's your great-grandmother's grave."

A thin granite headstone, so shallowly engraved that the letters were hard to read, but I managed. "Charity Garinch Tolan. Born 1879 in Humility, Massachusetts. Died this place in 1950."

So she'd had the same first name as my mother. And she and her daughter, my grandmother, had both been born in Massachusetts.

Peggy Crofton had come from Massachusetts. So had her cousin, Jack Payson.

I felt a darkening of my mood. Was this why I had feared to come here? Had I known in some subconscious fashion that I would find myself looking down at my great-grandmother's headstone—

An angry impatience with myself welled up. Why on earth was I attaching any significance to the fact that my great-grandmother, more than a hundred years ago, had been born in Massachusetts, the state that Peggy and her cousin Jack came from? Surely many hundreds of thousands of people over the generations had emigrated from Massachusetts to Connecticut. After all, the states had a common border.

I said, "Humility, Massachusetts. I wonder where it is."

"I don't know. The name intrigued me too, and so I tried to look it up on maps but couldn't find it. Perhaps it no longer exists."

"Perhaps."

I thanked him and walked through the gathering dusk to my car.

80

## ELEVEN

I GOT BEHIND the wheel and then looked at my watch. Not enough time now to prepare the dessert, charlotte russe, which I had planned for tonight. Well, no matter. I could buy two of those delicious-looking cherry tarts that Dilsey Wolsifer always displayed in her window. Since her cold reception of me my second day in Wessex, I had not been in her shop. But it was absurd to stay away. Hers was the only bakery in town. Surely I had as much right as anyone else to go there.

Besides, I wanted to ask her about my great-grandmother and my grandmother, and that Massachusetts town where they had been born.

I put the car in gear, drove to Main Street, and slid into a parking space a few doors from the bakery. I was in luck. There were no other customers inside the brightly lighted shop, only Dilsey, placing a tin of chocolate-covered doughnuts in the display counter.

The bell above the door tinkled as I entered. She straightened. What looked like alarm leaped into her eyes at sight of me. Then her face became expressionless.

"Hello, Dilsey."

She nodded.

"I'd like two cherry tarts, please."

Not speaking, she took a small cardboard box from the shelf behind her and placed it on the counter. She opened the back of the display case and, with a pair of tongs, transferred two tarts in their frilled paper cups to the box. "That'll be one-eighty."

I paid her. Then, as soon as she had rung up the money on the cash register: "There is something I want to ask you."

She just looked at me, waiting.

"You must have known my great-grandmother."

Unmistakable alarm in her eyes now. Her reply, when it came, was oblique. "She died a long time ago, before you were born."

"I know. It's on her tombstone. She died thirty-five years ago. You see, I was up at the Presbyterian churchyard today." I paused. "Do you know where it is, that Massachusetts town where both she and my grandmother were born?"

"No!"

"The Presbyterian minister doesn't know either. He said maybe it isn't in existence any longer."

"Maybe it isn't. Look, Linda." It was the first time since my return to Wessex that she had called me anything besides "you." She went on, "You're not going to be happy here, after what happened to your mother. Why don't you persuade that young husband of yours that you two should live in another town? He must still be crazy about you, married only a little while to a girl as pretty as you are."

"Why should I try to persuade him? Guy's people have lived here for three generations. He belongs here. And so do I, now that I'm his wife." My voice rose. "Why are you so unfriendly? Why do you want me to leave this town?"

She said, after a long moment, "I'm just thinking of your happiness."

"That's nonsense, and you know it. Why, you don't even like me." My throat tightened. "I don't know why. You liked me when I was little. I remember how you came to take care of me the morning after my mother—"

"I don't dislike you. I just think you'd be better off somewhere else. And if you do stay here—well, don't keep stirring about in the past."

"Stirring about in the past! Is that what you call visiting those three graves?"

She didn't answer but just looked at me, her lined face stubborn in the harsh glow of the overhead fluorescent light. Had she grown—well, peculiar with the years? That must be it.

At last she said, "If you don't mind, I'd like to close up now."

The small box in my hand, I went through the early darkness to my car. I laid the box on the seat and then hesitated.

Jack Payson might know something about that strangely named Massachusetts town. Anyway, his shop was only a few feet away, and it would do no harm to ask.

I could see no one at all in the Art Stall's interior, even though the lights were on and the cardboard sign inside the door's glass upper half said, "Open." I tried the knob. It didn't turn. Stuck, perhaps. I tapped on the glass, rattled the knob. I was just about to turn away when Jack opened the door at the rear of the shop and walked toward me.

He opened the front door and said, "My! Look what Santa brought me."

I stepped into the shop. "I was beginning to think you were closed."

"I am." He turned the dangling sign over. "Forgot to turn the sign over, that's all. But I'm always open to you, luv."

I ignored that. "I wondered if I could ask you something."

"Anything. But not down here. My dinner's in the oven and needs my attention. Come on."

He turned. After a moment I followed him down the length of the shop and up some narrow stairs. The apartment at the top, even though it consisted only of one large room, was attractive. Framed etchings of old Wessex houses hung on the plain white plaster walls. A dhurrie rug of muted red and blue was spread on the random-boarded pine floor. An Indian tree-of-life-patterned throw, which should have fought with the rug but didn't, covered a broad daybed. There were a pair of small armchairs covered in dark blue linen, and a nice old drop-leaf pine table and four pine dining chairs that looked to be genuine American antiques. A little alcove held a small range and a sink, with pine cupboards on the wall above them.

Jack hurried across the room, seized a red potholder affixed by a magnet to one side of the stove and opened the oven door. A sizzling sound and a delicious smell entered the room. He drew out a small aluminum baking pan that held a Rock Cornish hen, already nicely browned.

He spooned liquid in the pan over the bird. "Nothing like an orange glaze," he said.

"You do yourself proud."

He shrugged. "No point in living off take-out pizza just because I'm a bachelor. Say! I have an idea. Share this with me. I have a very nice Chablis I've been saving—"

"You know I can't. I'm going home in a few minutes to cook dinner for my husband."

He sighed. "Well, there I go again, the eternal optimist. I was hoping that he'd left you, or was in the hospital, or something. What are you cooking for the lucky stiff?"

I'd planned a crabmeat soufflé, but I knew it was best not to tell Jack Payson so. I might find myself exchanging recipes with him. "Just meat loaf and baked potatoes. Now what I wanted to ask you was—"

"Let's sit down."

We sat in the linen-covered armchairs. I said, "I was wondering just where you came from in Massachusetts."

"How nice of you to wonder. I was born in Boston. But not on Beacon Hill, alas, not even on the lower slopes."

"How about Peggy Crofton?"

"Where was she born, you mean? Mansfield, Massachusetts. What is this, dear? Some kind of survey?"

"No, not exactly. I mean—have you ever heard of Humility, Massachusetts?"

"Humility? Is that anywhere near Perspicacity?"

"Please, I'm serious."

"Sorry. No, I never heard of it. Should I have?"

"I thought you might have. My great-grandmother and my grandmother were born there. I went to the Presbyterian churchyard today and saw it on their tombstones."

Jack said nothing.

I went on, "The minister there says that he's tried to find the town on the maps, but couldn't. He says that maybe it's one of those tiny places that just disappeared. I guess he means after the mill folded, or whatever it was that kept the town going."

"I shouldn't wonder."

"Well, thank you, anyway." I stood up.

So did he. "You're not going!" His hands reached out and rested on my shoulders.

"I must. I'm late already."

Hands tightening on my shoulders, he smiled. "Knock it off, Linda."

"What do you mean, knock it—"

"Drop the coy act. We both know why you came here."

I tried to twist free of his grasp. "Let go of me! I came here because I wanted to know—"

"About some town in Massachusetts? If that was all you wanted you'd have come here in the daylight. You wouldn't have waited until I'd locked the door, and then knocked and rattled the knob until I came down to let you in."

Sheer anger held me motionless and mute for a moment. Men are my favorite sex, but there is one thing that some of them do that infuriates me. They blame their sexual aggressions on women. Something a woman said, or did, or wore, or didn't wear, was the same as "asking for it." It's been going on since Adam and Eve, and I hate it.

I jerked free of him, started for the stairs. He caught my shoulders and spun me around. Then, mouth on my mouth, arms binding my arms to my sides, he was pulling me toward the daybed.

I managed to draw one foot back and kick him in the shin. He'd been holding me too closely for me to give him a really strong kick, but apparently it was enough.

His arms dropped from me. He said, face flushed, eyes bright with rage, "Okay, Snow White. You can go now. Who needs you?"

I hurried down the stairs and along the length of the shop to the front door. I had trouble with the thumb latch but eventually it turned. Closing the door behind me, I went out into the night.

"Why, hello, Mrs. Nordeen."

Stunned with a sudden awareness that probably my lipstick was smeared and my hair disheveled, I looked at the woman who stood beside a car in the glow of a streetlamp, a bag of groceries in her arms. She was the plumber's wife, the woman I'd sat beside at the Ladies' Village Society meeting.

I said hello. Then I hurried to my own car, aware that by tomorrow it would be all over town that Guy Nordeen's wife of three months had visited Jack Payson after dark, and with the shop sign turned to "Closed."

APPARENTLY Guy did not hear of that visit to the Art Stall—not right away, that is. Our lives went on much as before, fairly calm on the surface but with tension underneath. Oh, we did have some pleasant hours together, enjoying our meals, and sharing TV programs, and making love. But far too often we snapped at each other over minor matters, or, what seemed to me worse, passed our hours together in silence. How had we, the young couple who'd fallen in love last summer in Venice, metamorphosed into this pair who, to judge by the way we behaved, might have had a decade of unsatisfactory marriage behind us?

The holiday season, celebrated Wessex style, brought a welcome distraction. A series of light snowfalls made the postcard-pretty village prettier than ever. Christmas carolers, looking self-consciously Dickensian in bright mufflers and caps, serenaded Main Street shoppers. Two evenings before Christmas, Ladies' Village Society members led those who had paid ten dollars for the privilege on a tour of a half-dozen fine old houses. Christmas Day, Guy and I went to the senior Nordeens, where a ten-foot balsam hung with old-fashioned ornaments—tiny drummer boys and wooden sleighs and farm animals—stood in one corner of the living room. Although my parents-in-law usually shunned ostentation, there was an ounce or two of Beluga caviar to accompany the champagne we sipped while we opened our presents. Guy's gift to me, incidentally, was a pair of amethyst earrings, the stones bordered by seed pearls; I gave him a calfskin attaché case.

All through the last half of December there were lots of parties. We too gave one the day after Christmas, a buffet dinner for twelve. One of the twelve was Peggy Crofton, whose New Year's Eve invitation we had already accepted. Although of course rather tense about playing a Wessex hostess for the first time, I did manage, with lobster Newburg and a duck galantine, to put my best culinary foot forward.

New Year's Eve at Peggy's was gala indeed, with everyone in evening dress, and a six-piece orchestra playing in the second-floor ballroom. In the small side room where I had found a few of the Village Society ladies gathered after the meeting that November day, a uniformed maid presided over racks of mink and blue fox and even a sable or two. As I looked around at the orchestra and at the bar where two bartenders dispensed drinks, I thought of the man whose money, twenty-odd years after his death, was paying for all this expensive festivity. Just why, I wondered fleetingly, had Hal Crofton shot himself?

That night I danced with almost every male guest, including Peggy's cousin Jack Payson. His dark face, stunningly handsome above a frilled evening shirt, at first gave no hint that he even remembered our stormy encounter in his one-room apartment. He asked polite questions about the state of my health and whether or not

89

I was painting. Then near the end of the number he asked, "Have you ever seen Peggy's library on the first floor?"

"No."

"She's probably the only woman in town with a full set of Anaïs Nin. What say you and I slip down there and browse for a while."

The orchestra stopped playing. "You never give up, do you?" I said.

He smiled. "No, but I also take precautions. Before I came here tonight I put on shin guards." He glanced over my shoulder. "Well, here comes old Colonel Baker, and from the gleam in his eye I can tell he's going to claim you for the next dance."

After the colonel, I danced with a tall, balding man who paid me extravagant compliments in a heavy French accent. His name was Jean-Paul Artois, he told me, and he was a yacht broker with "an international clientele."

As for Guy, he had danced the first dance after our arrival with me. But from then on he played the field. As the evening lengthened, though, he spent more and more time with Nicole Sorenson. She was wearing a silver lamé gown, a perfect foil for her artfully tousled dark hair. Seeing them dance together, I realized with a touch of dismay how beautifully their good looks contrasted, he wide-shouldered and blond, she small and slender and brunette.

A few minutes before twelve the band stopped playing, and someone turned a radio up to full volume. We listened to a voice follow the slow descent of the lighted ball above distant Times Square: "twenty-nine, twenty-eight, twenty-seven . . ."

I looked around, expecting to see Guy moving toward

90

me. Instead he stood with Nicole about twenty feet away. Both of them were smiling as they looked at the bandleader, standing with baton raised.

"—one! Happy New Year!"

All around me couples were kissing. I saw Guy bend to Nicole's proffered lips. It was not what one might call a lingering kiss, but neither was it brief. To my horror, I felt tears springing to my eyes. I managed to fight them back. Guy was coming toward me now. I found myself able to smile and to accept his kiss. But I could not repress the thought that tonight had seemed like a bad omen for the year ahead.

The next day several households dispensed eggnog and fruitcake, but after that the village grew quiet, as if exhausted by its annual orgy of festivity. Quite a few people went to Florida or Arizona or South America to spend the rest of the winter. Others, unable to escape the cold, made the most of it with ski weekends in New Hampshire and Vermont. As for me, I went to work on another book jacket, this one for a teenage book on forestry as a career. I wasn't too happy with the finished product, and I suspect the publishers weren't either, but they accepted it. I also went on with the task of furnishing the house, choosing carefully piece by piece.

My relations with Guy remained much as before, not really bad—we didn't shout or throw things—but a long way from the rewarding marriage that I had expected, and that I was sure he also had expected. In late March, with daffodil shoots already tall above the muddy earth, and the forsythia branches I'd brought into the house bursting into golden bloom, Guy began to bring work home with him several nights each week and shut himself up in one of the spare bedrooms. But at least he was working at *home*. As the winter passed I had begun to fear more and more the first evening he would call and say, "I won't be home until late, Linda. I'm having dinner with some out-of-town buyers."

Of course, I still might get that call from him. It was that nagging worry that, perhaps, one day in late March led me to make a potentially disastrous mistake. And I made it in the kitchen, the one place where I had always felt self-confident.

That morning a woman who had been one of the guests at our Christmas buffet telephoned me. The Episcopalian Church was having a bake sale. Even though I wasn't a member, could they count on me for some sort of pastry? I agreed, gladly. I loved to bake. And surely Guy, who from the first had urged me to "fit in," would be pleased. I drove to the supermarket and bought ingredients necessary for making my own version of individual Greek butter cakes.

The cleaning lady, Mrs. Carson, was there that morning. As I creamed sweet butter in the blender, I could also hear the whine of the vacuum cleaner in the dining room. I gradually added confectioner's sugar to the butter, then cinnamon and cloves, then an egg yolk. I picked up a small bottle, added a generous amount of brandy to the mixture, set the bottle down on the counter.

Suddenly Mrs. Carson spoke from a few feet behind me. "Mrs. Nordeen! What are you *doing?*"

Startled, I whirled around. Mrs. Carson's face, brown-skinned and thirtyish and attractive, held horror. "Look at that bottle you just used!"

I turned back, looked at the small bottle standing beside the blender. A wave of giddiness struck me. I clutched the counter edge to keep from falling.

92

It was not brandy I had added to the mixture. The brandy bottle stood a foot or so on the other side of the machine. What I had used was another brown liquid, poured from the bottle of brass cleaner I had been using earlier that morning on an antique lamp.

I switched off the machine. With a shaking hand I lifted the bottle. I of course had been aware that the label bore a skull and crossbones, but now I read the list of ingredients, including oxalic acid, and the words, "Poison! Can be fatal. If swallowed, call a physician immediately."

I thought of dozens of people here in Wessex, including my own parents-in-law perhaps, buying those little cakes of mine, cakes so highly spiced that those eating them might not even realize that there was something wrong with the taste, not until it was too late.

How had I, an experienced cook, made such a ghastly error? Why had I even left the bottle of brass cleaner out on the counter, instead of putting it away in the cabinet beneath the sink?

If Mrs. Carson hadn't walked into the kitchen just then, Guy might indeed have had good reason to regret having married me and brought me to his hometown.

A sound of squealing wheels as Mrs. Carson pushed the high counter stool toward me. "You'd better sit down, Mrs. Nordeen."

I sank onto the stool. I said, dry mouthed, "I'll never be able to thank you enough. My God, if you hadn't been here—" Then, to my dismay, I heard myself blurt out, "I think it's this house. It—"

I broke off. She said, after a moment, "Ma'am?"

"It's nothing. I mean, it's just a feeling I get every once in a while. Pay no attention."

She stood for a moment with an indecisive look on her

face and then said, "So you don't like this house either."

Startled, I just looked at her.

She went on, "I like you, Mrs. Nordeen. But to tell you the truth, I don't like coming to this house. I don't know why. It's certainly a fine-looking house, and new, and easy to work in. But just the same—"

When I didn't respond, she said, "I know it's none of my business. But if you don't like this house, why don't you tell Mr. Nordeen you want to live somewhere else?"

"I can't," I said dully. "There's nothing wrong that you can put your finger on. I can't say that the house is inconvenient, or too dark, or too drafty. It's none of those things. Besides, my father-in-law built it. Instead of selling it at a good profit, the way he'd planned, he's letting us live here at a very reasonable rent. How can I say I don't like the place?"

"Well, I guess maybe you can't." She was silent for a moment. Then she said, "I'd better go, Mrs. Nordeen. I'm due at my next place."

I got up and went to the breakfast table, where I'd left my handbag. With shaking fingers I took bills from my wallet and held them out to her.

"Mrs. Carson."

"Yes, ma'am?"

"Please don't tell anyone." I meant, please don't tell anyone I came near to poisoning dozens of people.

Her dark eyes were filled with sympathy. "I won't, Mrs. Nordeen. I won't tell even my husband or my daughters."

She left then. I put the brass cleaner where it belonged, under the sink. I emptied that lethal mixture I had concocted down the disposal. I took the blender apart and scalded it. Then, hands still shaking, I set about making

94

another batch of cookies—brownies this time. I felt that never again would I make Greek butter cakes.

I'm sure Mrs. Carson kept her promise to remain silent. I could see no change in the attitude of the townspeople toward me. But I remained shaken for days.

Then, in mid-April, everything changed for me. I began to be almost certain that I was pregnant. I felt a joyful thanksgiving. Surely now whatever afflicted my relationship with Guy would vanish. But I did not want to tell him right away of my hopes. Better to wait until I was sure, I told myself, although in my heart I knew that what held me back from confiding in him was the fear that he would not share my joy.

I wouldn't even go to a Wessex doctor, I decided, lest Guy hear of it. Instead I could call up a Hartford gynecologist, a woman whose name I'd heard mentioned at a Ladies' Village Society meeting. After all, I'd planned anyway to go into Hartford later in the week for a sale of oriental rugs I'd seen advertised. I'd always felt a little nervous about what might happen to that antique Kerman, the property of the senior Nordeens, which covered our living-room floor.

On Thursday I drove into Hartford and kept my appointment with the gynecologist. She confirmed my pregnancy. Feeling almost dizzy with mingled joy and trepidation, I left her office. Out on the sunny sidewalk, I looked at my watch. Almost one. I would have lunch—a celebratory lunch; no McDonald's for me today!—before going to the rug place. I walked a block to La Pompadour, a fashionable restaurant I knew only by reputation.

La Pompadour was one of those places where the management, for mysterious reasons, keeps the illumination so dim that they really should equip their waiters with flashlights, like movie ushers. Nevertheless, I managed to follow my waiter to a small table against one wall. He handed me a menu about the size of a pillow slip and walked away. The hand-printed bill of fare was in such large letters that even in that light I could read it. I decided on sole with white grapes and spring asparagus. Then I laid the menu aside and, now that my eyes had adjusted to the dimness, looked around me.

Do you know "Guess Who I Saw Today," a ballad much favored by café singers? I think Nancy Wilson often sings it. Anyway, it was just like the song.

Guy and Nicole Sorenson were seated at a table in the center of the room. Irrelevantly, I wondered if the maître d' had placed them conspicuously because they were such a handsome couple. With coffee cups in front of them, they sat, not saying anything at the moment, just smiling at each other.

Was it a coincidence? On the same day that I had reason to treat myself to this expensive place, had they just happened to run into each other on the street and then decided to lunch together? Oh, that was possible. But it seemed to me far more probable, from the way they smiled at each other, that they had lunched together often.

But they could scarcely be having an affair, I told myself desperately. After all, Guy still came home before dinner every night.

And then I thought of what someone has called that great American institution, the afternoon shackup. I thought of those motel ads: "Bring romance back into your life! Every room equipped with TV and private bar! Only minutes from the business district!"

I felt sick, sick. I fumbled in my handbag for my wallet,

dropped a bill onto the table, shoved my chair back. On my way out I met my waiter.

"But, Madame!"

"Not feeling well," I said.

In the doorway to the café's anteroom I looked back. Plainly neither of them had seen me. They were still smiling at each other.

## THIRTEEN

WHILE I was driving toward Wessex on the interstate, the car ahead of me suddenly slowed, and I, lost in my frightened and bitter thoughts, came within inches of hitting it. After that I tried to get hold of myself. I must not give way to emotion. Instead I must think as clearly and calmly as possible.

One thing was obvious. I must not vent my furious hurt on Guy, not if I wanted to hold my marriage together, and I did want to, now more than ever. I must not even let him know I had seen him with Nicole today.

I stopped at the supermarket and bought a number of items, including lamb chops and new potatoes for that night's dinner. When I reached the house, I went in the back way. With the bag of groceries still in my arms, I stood in the middle of the kitchen floor and listened. No sound. Even a flock of newly arrived grackles, who had been giving their creaky-gate calls as I crossed the back lawn, were silent now.

It's this house, I thought. This house murders happiness, murders love.

But I knew that was crazy. It wasn't the house, this newly assembled structure of wood and sheet rock and fiberglass. It was me. Apparently I was the sort of woman that men deceive. First, although he hadn't mattered much, that married man. And now there was Guy, who mattered more than I would have believed possible.

Still, if my husband and I could get away from this house, away from Wessex, for a little while, it might just possibly make a difference.

By the time Guy came home I was fairly calm, at least outwardly. Because the evening had turned cool, I had built a small fire in the living room grate. As he sat beside it, sipping his scotch and water, he seemed tired and preoccupied, very different indeed from the man I'd seen smiling at his pretty luncheon companion only a few hours earlier. I wanted to shout at him, "You've got to straighten up! You're going to be a father!" But I'd already had that out with myself. I didn't want to use our baby that way, even though it might be the surest way of holding onto him. A baby ought to be wanted by both its parents. And surely a man must feel resentment toward a child who kept him locked in an unwanted marriage, no matter how he might try to hide that resentment, even from himself.

And so, if I had lost Guy's love, I had to get it back, somehow. And I had to do it all on my own, if I possibly could.

I said, "Guy, couldn't we go away someplace for a little while?"

He looked startled. "Away? This time of year?"

"Just for a week or ten days. I'm sure you and your father could rearrange your work schedule. And I think we both need to get away."

A little flicker in his eyes. Was he wondering if I had guessed something? He asked, "Where would you want to go?"

"New York. I'd like to see some publishers there."

He said slowly. "And there are some customers I could call on."

"You see? Oh, Guy! And let's not even tell Aunt Ellen and Uncle Brad we're there, at least not until near the end of our stay. I'd like this to be—just for us."

"All right." He gave a rather forced-looking smile. "I guess I can manage ten days. When would you want to leave?"

"This weekend?"

"Okay. This weekend."

I had almost forgotten how beautiful New York can be in the spring. Masses of tulips blooming along the Park Avenue mall. Brisk breezes whipping the scalloped canopies in front of apartment houses. Trees in side streets showing the first tender green leaves. And in Central Park, flowering crab apple and cherry and quince, and great drifts of daffodils.

From the balcony of our room high in a Fifth Avenue hotel, Guy and I could see the sweep of Central Park from the reservoir to the zoo and even farther south. We could see the bicyclists, and the children and dogs playing on the hills, and the carriage horses drawing loads of tourists along the curving roads at a brisk clip.

But for me the greatest beauty of that interlude in New York was what happened to Guy and me.

It started when we were only a few miles from Wessex. Aware of his glance, I turned to him.

"Hello, Linda." He smiled. One of his hands left the wheel to grasp my hand. "You look like a teenager on her way to her first prom."

I wanted to say, I hope I'm on my way to something

100

better than that, much, much better. But all I did was to lean my head against his shoulder.

We reached our Fifth Avenue hotel in midafternoon. Guy finished his unpacking first and then sat watching me as I moved back and forth between my suitcase, opened out on the luggage stand, and the sliding-door closet. At last I said, "There, that's finished! Now what shall we do first? You know what I'd like to do? I'd like to go to the seal pool in the park. All the time I was growing up, I visited the seals at least once a week."

Guy stood up and drew me close to him. "Later," he said. "We'll visit the seals later."

We crammed so much into those ten days. Guy called on his customers, and I discussed future work with a publisher's art department head, but aside from that we devoted ourselves entirely to pleasure. We went to the theater, shunning by tacit agreement the problem dramas in favor of musicals and comedies. We went to restaurants all over town, including some trendy West Side places where the customers apparently liked being packed in so tightly they could scarcely wield their knives and forks, let alone hear each other speak. We went to discos, including one patronized by punk rockers with green or magenta hair and with safety pins dangling from their earlobes. When I expressed surprise that the two muscular doormen had let us in, Guy grinned and said, "It's because we're dressed so funny." We lunched at a sidewalk café on an especially warm day and then boarded a steamer for the trip around Manhattan's gleaming towers.

And we made love, many times. For me, and I think for Guy also, the experience seemed as new and wonderful as it had on that Caribbean island.

I thought of Nicole now and then. But more and more I felt that my own worst fears had been unfounded. Guy had not been having an affair with Nicole, or even contemplating one. Guy loved *me*.

It must have been coincidence, after all. The day that I saw them together, he must have run into her on the street and asked her to lunch. Of course he'd been enjoying himself when I saw him. What healthy young man wouldn't enjoy lunching with a girl that pretty? And what girl wouldn't be pleased to have lunch with Guy? But it hadn't meant anything important.

Toward the end of our stay in New York, I had some confirmation of my growing belief that there was nothing to worry about. As we walked beside a Central Park bridle path one afternoon, after a visit to the seal pond, a girl astride a bay horse passed us. "Did you notice that girl?" Guy asked. "She looked like Nicole Sorenson."

My pulse gave a nervous leap. "Nicole is prettier, I'd say."

He nodded. "She's pretty, all right, and a nice kid. If you ask me, she's way too good for that phony Frenchman she's so crazy about."

"What phony Frenchman?"

"Oh, I suppose he's French, all right. But I doubt that he has a title, the way he keeps hinting."

"What's his name?"

"Jean-Paul Artois. You probably met him at Peggy Crofton's New Year's Eve party. Tall guy, very thin. About forty."

I did remember him then, although not too clearly. That night most of my attention had been taken up by the fact that Guy danced several times with Nicole.

"He calls himself a yacht broker," Guy went on, "although I think professional house guest would be a better

102

description. Whenever he's in Wessex he stays with Irene Blaisdell." Mrs. Blaisdell, a neighbor of Peggy Crofton's, was the elderly widow of an investment banker. "I hear he's down in the Bahamas now, staying with some middle-aged soft-drink heiress, but I'm sure he'll be back in Wessex before long."

I said, feeling as if the spring sunlight had grown even a shade brighter, "Do you think Nicole wants to marry him?"

"I'm sure of it. A guy like that must seem big romantic stuff to a girl Nicole's age."

We crossed Fifth Avenue then, and had a midafternoon drink in a bar, Campari for Guy and tomato juice for me. Because of my pregnancy, I drank nothing alcoholic during those days in New York. At first I'd half feared, half hoped that Guy would guess the reason for my abstemiousness. But when I'd told him that New York itself was "turn-on enough for me," he'd just smiled and taken my word for it.

I didn't call the Cartwrights until the day before we were to leave. Aunt Ellen answered the phone. "Darling! How long have you been in town?"

"More than a week. Please don't feel hurt that I didn't call you earlier. I'll explain when I see you."

"You'd better. But if you'll come to dinner tonight, I'll forgive you ahead of time."

That evening, once the dinner table was cleared, Aunt Ellen and I left the men to a Yankee–Red Sox game on TV and went into my old room for a chat. I explained why we hadn't telephoned earlier.

"I felt we needed some time completely to ourselves. We haven't been getting along too well. Nothing too important. Just minor irritations and so on."

I wasn't being consciously deceptive. By now I had

103

come to feel that Guy's troubles and mine had been no more than minor.

Aunt Ellen nodded wisely. "The first year is often full of stresses."

"I felt we needed a second honeymoon, and I was right. It's been wonderful."

I told her then that I was expecting a child in October. She embraced and kissed me.

"How wonderful. I'll bet Guy is thrilled to pieces."

"He doesn't know yet."

"Doesn't know! He's to be a father next fall and he doesn't—"

"I'll tell him as soon as we get home. But I wanted this time in New York to be what it turned out to be, a second honeymoon."

She smiled. "Maybe you're right. Hearing the news will be a fine homecoming present for him."

## FOURTEEN

I N OUR hotel room the day before we left New York, we had heard a radio broadcast about a wind-and-rain storm in southern Connecticut. Even so, as we drove down Main Street Sunday evening we were surprised to see some shop windows boarded over. And when we turned into our driveway we were both startled and dismayed to see part of a tree limb protruding from a living room window.

"Damn!" Guy said. "Wouldn't you think that Dad would have gotten somebody over here to board up that window?"

"Maybe he hasn't been by here."

"He should have checked up, after a windstorm like that. Well, I just hope a lot of rain didn't get in."

But a lot had. That beautiful antique Kerman was not only rain-soaked but strewn with sticky buds from the horse-chestnut branch that had shattered the window.

Guy carried our bags upstairs and then came back down to wrestle the tree branch out onto the lawn. I cleaned up the mess on the rug as best I could. Then while Guy went back to the garage to find something to put over the window, I went to the kitchen and took a container of supermarket chicken with noodles from the freezer. No gourmet meal tonight. Neither of us would appreciate it, not after the long drive through weekend traffic and then the discovery of the wind damage. As I stood at the kitchen counter, slicing tomatoes and listening to the sound of Guy's hammer, I began to feel a familiar deflation of my spirit creeping over me. Later, while I set the dining-room table, I heard Guy out in the hall telephoning his father about the broken window. He sounded accusatory, and as nearly as I could tell from hearing only one end of the conversation, the elder Nordeen had responded in kind.

"Oh, sure," Guy said. "I know my going off to New York left you with more work, but surely you could have taken a few minutes to drive over here—"

Mr. Nordeen must have said something then, because Guy responded, "Well, if you've both been feeling below par, that's different. Now how did that hassle over the Whittaker account come out?—They did!—Yes, I know I'd been the one dealing with them, but I still don't see why my being away for a few days should have mattered that much."

Because we'd gone away, an extremely valuable rug had been badly damaged and, apparently, another Nordeen Importers client had been alienated in one way or another. I wondered wretchedly if Guy was beginning to regret those ten golden days. No, surely not. It was too bad that the rug was harmed and the client miffed, but the renewal of our love had been worth it many times over.

I went into the living room. With one window boarded up and the light outside fading rapidly, the room had a gloomy look. A fire would help. Because I sensed that Guy would be in no mood for building a fire, I myself put crumpled newspaper and kindling and three small logs in the grate. Right here, beside the fire, I'd tell him about the baby. And after that, a damaged Kerman and a disgruntled client would not seem so important.

We had predinner drinks beside the fire, scotch and water for him and plain soda for me, although Guy may have thought there was vodka in it. Since he made no comment, I couldn't tell.

After a while I said, "I've got news for you."

Frowning, he lifted his abstracted gaze from the flames. "What did you say?"

"I have news for you. Guy, we're going to have a baby."

For a moment he stared at me as if I had been speaking Urdu. Then he said, "When?"

"Late October."

"When did you find out?"

"About two weeks ago."

Those very blue eyes stared at me for a long, long moment. "You've known for two weeks, and you didn't tell me?"

Because I saw you with Nicole, I wanted to say. I was afraid I was losing you, and I wanted to win you back, all on my own, without any form of emotional blackmail.

But I didn't want to say that, didn't want to risk a quarrel, tonight of all nights, and so I said nothing.

"Well?"

"Does it matter? I'm telling you now."

"Damned right it matters! Why the two weeks' silence?" Then in an even voice: "Were you getting up your courage?"

I cried, "Courage! What on earth—"

"It would certainly take a kind of courage for a woman to tell her husband what you'd just told me—that is, if the baby was another man's."

I said, momentarily stupified, "What other man?"

"Jack Payson, of course. I don't think there have been

any others. If there had been I'd have heard about it in a town this size. But I did hear that you were seen coming out of Payson's place one night, with your hair and your clothes and your makeup all messed up. I didn't say anything then because I didn't want to believe it. I told myself that maybe some jealous old biddy—"

His voice trailed off. I stared at him, unable to speak or move. He said, "The New York trip was to soften me up, wasn't it? You thought I'd come back so crazy about you that it would never occur to me to wonder—"

That strange paralysis left me. I sprang to my feet, hurled the contents of my glass into his face and ran toward the stairs.

I was in our bedroom, with the door locked, by the time he too came up the stairs. He pounded on the door. "Linda! Unlock this door!"

"Go away," I said. "Go to hell and burn there."

"Linda, if you don't open this door—"

"You'll do what? What can you do to me that's worse than what you've already done tonight?"

"Linda—"

"You could break the door down and beat me up. But what would your parents say, and your customers, and this whole town?"

Silence for a while. Then I heard him turn away, go down the stairs. Several minutes passed. Then I heard the distant sounds of the back door opening, closing. I heard the Mustang start up, back down the drive.

I stood there for an interval. Then I went down to the kitchen. I turned off the oven, took out the now blackened chicken-and-noodles concoction, and emptied the aluminum container into the garbage disposal. I did the same with the tomato and lettuce salad. Then I returned to the bedroom.

108

I COULDN'T HAVE been asleep for more than two hours when the ringing of the bedside phone dragged me back to consciousness. Early daylight filled the room. Knowing who the caller must be, I reached out, lifted the phone, and said hello.

"Linda." Guy sounded miserable and very, very tired.

"Where are you calling from? Your parents' house?"

"No, the Nutmeg Inn." That was a motel about a mile south of the village limits. "Linda, can you ever forgive me?"

"I don't know. Perhaps. But not right away."

"I don't know why I behaved like that. Well, I do know. It still seems strange that you didn't tell me about the baby as soon as you yourself knew."

I told him then what I had chosen not to tell him the night before. That expensive Hartford restaurant. He and Nicole, smiling at each other across the table. "I thought I was losing you." My voice sounded as flat and tired as his. "And I didn't want to use the baby to try to hold onto you. I wanted to—to make you fall in love with me all over again."

"Oh, Linda, Linda! I was never out of love with you. Oh, things didn't seem to be going too well between us,

109

not as well as I'd hoped for. But they were never so bad that—"

He broke off, and then went on, "As for Nicole, she'd been to see me earlier that day on an errand for Peggy. Something about an eighteenth-century Venetian glass chandelier that Peggy wants for her entrance hall. I asked Nicole to lunch. She spent most of the meal talking about Jean-Paul."

"From the way you two were looking at each other—"

"Don't you see how you could read too much into that, just because things hadn't been going smoothly for us? Oh, hell. Probably I was looking—appreciative. What guy wouldn't appreciate Nicole? But it was nothing more than that."

I remained silent, turning his words over in my mind.

After a moment he went on, "And maybe in much the same way, I made too much of the Jack Payson business. But you see, I heard you'd been seen coming out of his place, looking as if you'd been in a wrestling match—"

"I had been, in a way. He made a pass, a strenuous one, and I kicked him in the shin and ran. I didn't tell you because I was afraid of what you might do about it. Too, I felt guilty, since you'd already warned me what sort he was. But ever since then I've had nothing to do with him, except to dance with him once on New Year's Eve."

After several seconds he said, "I believe you. But last night, when I learned you'd kept the baby a secret from me, you can see how I'd remember that story about you and Payson, and think that maybe—"

"Yes," I said wearily, "I can see." But it was our lack of trust in each other, a trust we should have achieved by now, which had led us both to leap to wrong conclusions.

"I'll come home now, darling. We'll have breakfast and drink a toast to the baby, in orange juice."

"No."

"What do you mean, no?"

"I think we should be apart for a while, at least a couple of weeks. There's something wrong with our marriage, Guy, something fundamental. I want to think about it."

He argued for a few minutes, but I could tell from a flatness in his voice that he agreed with me about there being something basically wrong with our relationship. At last he said, in that dispirited voice, "You'll need the car. I'll rent one for myself. And you've got your own checkbook."

"Yes."

"I'll go on staying here at the motel. Less hassle that way. If I stay with my parents, I'll have to keep trying to explain things to Mother."

"I understand."

"Don't you want to talk to me at all while we're staying apart, Linda? Face to face, I mean."

"Not now. In a few days perhaps, but not now."

"All right," he said heavily. "Will you pack a bag for me? Leave it on the front porch. I'll pick it up in an hour or less."

About forty-five minutes later, I looked down through the curtains of the bedroom window and saw the Mustang turn into the driveway. A following car, a dark blue convertible with its top up, had stopped at the curb out front. A young black man sat at the wheel. The rental car, obviously.

Guy got out of the Mustang, walked toward the house entrance. Momentarily he disappeared from my view. Then he was out in the driveway again, carrying the suitcase I'd packed. Plainly he realized I must be watching from behind the curtain, because he stood there with his

111

face upturned to the morning sunlight. He looked pale and puzzled and weary, like the considerably older brother of the young man with whom I'd shared that Fifth Avenue hotel room.

My whole heart yearned toward him. I wanted to cry, "Don't go!" but I must not, for his sake, and my own, and our child's. I had to think things through, had to decide whether I should try to go on living with Guy here in Wessex, or should insist that he pull up roots three generations deep and move away, or, indeed, should stay with him at all.

He turned finally and walked toward the car waiting at the curb.

## SIXTEEN

THE NEXT few days were like a dream, a bad one. Outdoors, the Connecticut spring was golden with daffodils, fragrant with the first lilacs, and loud with the singing of birds. Inside the house there was silence—an odd, dead silence—unless I kept radio music and talk shows on, which I did much of the time. On Wednesday a glazier, sent by Guy, showed up to repair that living room window. Otherwise no one visited the house.

With my gynecologist's permission—"Only don't overdo it!"—I resumed my early-morning runs, although they did not bring me the highs that jogging often had in the past. In that room over the garage, I tried to work on the cover assignment that a New York publisher had given me. It was for another teenage book, one on truck gardening. The work didn't go well, and finally I abandoned it. I'd go back to it later, I told myself. The cover wasn't due for another month. After stopping work on the cover, I spent my time with books or the TV set, absorbing little of what I read or saw, and with household tasks. Using a bottled rug cleaner I worked, very cautiously, on the stained Kerman. The stain did not come out. I knew that perhaps I should send the rug to a Hartford cleaner who specialized in orientals, but I didn't want to do so without my mother-in-law's permission. And of course I didn't want to call her. The very fact that she, who usually called me every day or so for a brief chat, had remained silent made me realize that Guy must have told his parents of our trouble and asked them to stay clear.

All the time, of course, I was trying to think through my problems with Guy. I got no place. There seemed to be nothing to grasp. If the problem had been that either he or I drank too much, I could have decided that he—or I—must join AA. If the problem had been money, I might have thought, "A sensible budget is the answer." If we'd had in-law trouble, I might have concluded that we must tell our relations, if necessary in so many words, that they must not interfere in our marriage. But the problem was nothing so concrete as alcohol or money or in-laws. What was it, some sort of personality clash? I only knew that somehow, except for short periods of time, Guy and I had not found the happiness that should be the lot of a couple who were young and prosperous and in love.

Sometimes I wondered if it were all my fault. Perhaps, because of my traumatic childhood experience here, I had come to Wessex with a subconscious certitude that we could not be happy here. No, worse than that. Perhaps I had harbored a *will* for our marriage to fail. Perhaps that was why I had let Jack Payson, even though I knew what he was, persuade me to come with him up to his living quarters that night. Looking back now, it seemed to me that I should have forseen the possible consequences—gossip that would reach my husband and, even though he might not challenge me about it right then, would plant a seed of suspicion in his mind.

Often during those solitary days, I wondered if I should

114

not just give up. File for divorce, go to New York, and raise my child by myself. I would be better off than many single mothers. I had a salable talent. And surely Guy would pay generous child support—unless, I thought bleakly, he decided that the child wasn't his after all. Often during those days, I was conscious of no coherent thought, just a kind of numbness as I moved through a house that, despite sounds pouring from the TV set or radio, seemed to hold a heavy silence.

I did not spend all of my time in the house, of course. I went to the supermarket, and the laundromat, and the bank. From the way people greeted me, poorly masked curiosity in their eyes, I knew they had heard that Guy wasn't living at home these days. No one made any reference to the situation, though, not even Guy's great and good friend Peggy Crofton when I met her just outside the bank one day. ("You will come to our next meeting, won't you?" she said, and I answered, "I'll try," although I knew that wild horses couldn't drag me to a meeting of about forty women of the town, all of them wondering about me.)

On Saturday I caught a glimpse of Peggy's niece, Nicole. As I stepped out of one of the town's two drugstores, I saw her driving past in her red sports car. Jean-Paul Artois sat beside her, looking too tall for the little car. So the Frenchman was back in town, just as Guy had predicted. Apparently, though, his reunion with Nicole had not been an entirely happy one. The Frenchman's bony face had a set look, both stubborn and uneasy, and Nicole appeared on the verge of tears.

I saw Nicole the next day, too. But this time she wasn't with Jean-Paul. She was with my husband.

That morning, a Sunday, had dawned cloudy and

115

threatening, but shortly past noon the sky cleared and the day, although still brisk, became bright. Abandoning thoughts of trying to get back to work on that book cover, I changed to a dark green velour sweat shirt and pants. Through the Sabbath hush I ran down to the road that paralleled the river, turned right, and then right again along the woodland road where, that stormy day, Jack Payson had stopped and picked me up in his Bentley. With a pang I saw that it would not be a woodland road much longer. A line of sewer pipe lay just beyond a ditch at the road's edge, and a few house lots had already been cleared of trees.

I had run perhaps half a mile along that road when my right ankle turned. It was the most minor of injuries, one that couldn't even be called a sprain. Still, it might be wise to give my ankle a brief rest before I went on. Just ahead a wide plank bridged the newly excavated ditch. I crossed it and sat down on one of the lengths of sewer pipe.

It was pleasant there in the sunlight and in the soon-to-be-destroyed woodland, so pleasant that for a blessed interval I was aware only of the sunlight on my face and hands and of the *dee-dee-dee* birdcall that I had learned to identify as the chickadee's. Soon one of the charming little birds flew from the woods behind me to perch a foot or so away from me on the pipe, cocking its black head first to one side and then the other. Bold and perpetually hungry, like all of its kind, it hoped for a handout. "I'm sorry," I said. "If I'd known I was to stop here I'd have brought sunflower seeds." The bird seemed to ponder my words for a moment and then flew off. I clasped one knee and turned my face up to the sun.

The sound of a car, moving slowly. I opened my eyes.

It came into view, a dark blue convertible, its top down on this bright afternoon. A second later I saw, with an almost painful contraction of my heart, that Guy was behind the wheel. Nicole sat beside him. She was crying, her curly dark head bent, her pretty face distorted. I saw Guy reach out and draw the weeping girl against his shoulder.

Even if they'd looked in my direction, probably they wouldn't have seen me, with my dark green warm-up suit blending into the trees and underbrush. But neither of them did look.

I gazed after the car. It could be, I told myself, that it meant very little, no more than that luncheon in Hartford had. Nicole had been unhappy, in all probability because of Jean-Paul. She had run into Guy somewhere, or perhaps even called him at the motel in hope of a friendly ear and a comforting shoulder.

But the situation was more dangerous now than it had been at the time of that Hartford luncheon. Now Guy and I, at least temporarily, were living apart. And Nicole, plainly, was miserable. It would be far from the first time that two people had decided to pool their separate forms of unhappiness in hope of achieving its opposite.

After a while I recrossed the plank and, favoring my right ankle, started back to the house.

Four more days passed. Then on Friday, as I lay in bed around eight o'clock, debating whether or not to get up just yet to another day in this silent house, the bedside phone rang. Hoping in spite of myself that I would hear Guy's voice, I picked up the phone and said hello.

"Mrs. Nordeen? This is Miss Hernshaw."

After a moment I said, embarrassed, "Forgive me, but I'm afraid I don't recall exactly—"

117

"You talked to me the day you came to visit Sara Breed at the hospital in Claverly."

"Oh, of course. Forgive me, Miss Hernshaw."

"That's all right. Sara wants to see you, Mrs. Nordeen, although she calls you Mrs. Edwards, I mean, she still has you confused with your mother."

"Why does she—"

"She says you promised to come back to see her. And now she says that there is something more she wants to tell you, something important. We're really having quite a time with her. And so if it isn't too much trouble—"

Why not, I thought wearily. True, there was little chance that anything Sara Breed might say would make sense. But still, she just might be able to tell me more about that night when my mother had met her death in that moonlit pool.

Besides, what else did I have to do with the day ahead of me?

"When shall I come?"

"Early afternoon, if that's convenient for you. Things are pretty hectic around here from late morning through lunchtime."

"All right. I'll be there around one-thirty."

## SEVENTEEN

I T WAS a gray afternoon. As I sat waiting in that small visiting room, a few big raindrops ran a crooked course down the windowpane inside the heavy black bars. It struck me that the drops looked like desultory tears.

The door opened and a nurse's aide, a different one than I'd seen during my first visit here, brought Sara into the room. The coarse-featured face lit up at sight of me. "Hello, missus!" She said nothing more until the door had closed behind the aide. Then, seated close to me in one of the chintz-covered chairs, she leaned forward.

"Missus, I got to tell you something. I didn't tell you last time because I was scared, but nothing bad happened to me for what I did tell you, so—"

Her words took a disconcerting leap. "And anyway, maybe they ain't so strong. They wanted you dead, and you ain't, are you?"

I said tautly, "Sara—"

"I been afraid maybe they could get at me, even in here. But nothing bad's happened since the last time you was here, so I'm going to tell you the rest of it."

"The rest of it? About the voices, you mean?"

"Yes. I *seen* them, missus."

"You saw —"

119

"The people who put the voices in my head. I seen them at night, in the woods."

So much for my hope that she might have something factual to tell me, rather than just more fancies of a mind that, never strong, apparently had fallen into complete disorder back there almost eighteen years ago.

"Oh, Sara!" The tone of my own voice awakened a memory. My mother used to sound like that when Sara did or said something unreasonable.

"I *seen* them, missus. They didn't see me, not the first time. They was standing in a circle and singing, only it was more like talking. And they had long coats with something that come up over their heads."

She stopped speaking, little gray eyes fixed earnestly on my face. I said, "You mean they were wearing cloaks, with hoods?"

She must have seen something like that on TV, hooded figures standing in a circle in a nighttime wood. Yes, that was surely it.

Nevertheless, in this plain little room, with a radiator clanking as the heat came up, I felt a shiver down my spine.

"I dunno what you'd call them, missus, but with those things over their heads I couldn't see their faces. They was holding candles in their hands, too.

"I got away without them knowing the first time," Sara went on. "But the second time when I was trying to sneak off I stumbled on something and I fell down. And they caught me."

Dark figures converging on a heavy-bodied woman who was really a child. Again, even though I was sure that the event had no reality outside her mind, I felt that ripple down my spine again.

120

"What did they do to you, Sara?"

Uncertainty in the broad face now. "I couldn't tell you rightly, missus. I guess I went to sleep."

"Went to sleep!"

"Yes. When I woke up it was still dark, and they was gone. So I ran back to the house."

"You mean you realize those people were just a dream?"

"Oh, no, missus! They was real. And they got inside my head, somehow. All the time I was running back to the house they kept telling me I'd die if I ever told I seen them. And later on they told me about the white powder on my closet shelf—" She gave a whimper. "Oh, missus! I'm so sorry for what I done."

"I know you are, Sara." I hesitated, and then gave way to a sudden curiosity as to what sort of setting she had constructed for her nightmarish fantasy. "Now you said you never went 'up there' again. Where was up there?"

She looked blank.

"Where was it you saw the people standing in a circle?"

"Oh! A long ways from the house. Not toward the pool where I—the other way. It was up by that tree that was all white. You told me lightning musta struck it."

Her voice quickened. "We was up there together once, missus. It was the day Linda got lost. We found her asleep up there."

Memory stirred. I couldn't have been much more than five the day I wandered off into the woods and couldn't find my way back. I recall running one way and then the other, tears streaming down my face, through woods where sunlight slanted down through trees that seemed to me mile-high. I don't remember coming to a small

121

clearing, or curling up at the foot of a lightning-blasted pine, but I do remember coming awake there in sunset light, with my frantic-faced mother kneeling beside me and Sara standing a few feet away, a broad, relieved smile on her face.

"You remember, missus?"

"I remember."

"Did I ask you about Linda the last time you was here?"

"Yes. Linda's fine."

I looked over her shoulder at the door. Sara could talk with me for fifteen minutes, Miss Hernshaw had said. Surely that much time had passed. I wanted to get away. Somehow Sara's reference to the bleached skeleton of that pine tree had made her fantasy seem almost real to me.

"You'll bring Linda next time you come?"

I said, after a moment, "I'll try."

To my relief the door in the far wall opened and the nurse's aide came in. "Time to say good-bye, Sara."

Sara threw the aide a wary glance and then asked, in a low voice, "Did I do right to tell you, missus?"

"You did."

A broad smile spread across her face. "Good-bye, missus," she said, and let the aide lead her out.

I went through the other door, the one that led into the hall. Miss Hernshaw had asked me to drop by her office before I left. I tapped on her door and went in.

Briefly I told her of Sara's account of hooded figures. "Do you think that she has seen something about witches on TV lately?"

"Good heavens, no! Our patients watch TV, of course. In fact, TV is such a help in keeping them content that I

122

sometimes wonder what mental institutions did before it was invented. But we show them only material that we have previously taped. We do our best to make sure they don't watch anything disturbing."

"I can understand that."

"But that doesn't mean that she couldn't have seen such a movie on TV or in a theater twenty years ago, or even forty years ago, when she was still a child. Psychiatrists have traced some schizophrenic delusions to nightmares the patients suffered when only four or five. Her doctor will be very interested in what you told me. Oh, don't worry," she said, as I started to protest. "She'll never know you told us. Obviously she's afraid of some sort of reprisal for confiding in you, and of course we will do nothing to increase her fears."

## EIGHTEEN

WHEN I emerged from the hospital I found that the fitful rain seemed to have stopped entirely, although the sun was still obscured by a gray overcast, with remnants of darker clouds scudding beneath it. I drove out of the long hospital drive and turned toward Wessex.

I had thought that once I was away from that cheerless place I could turn my attention to other matters. But the scene Sara Breed had described stayed before me, almost as if she had managed to project her delusions into my own supposedly sane mind. Instead of the traffic, and the asphalt road still wet with rain, I kept seeing the nighttime wood, and candlelight that didn't touch hooded faces.

I felt an increasing anger with myself. Didn't I have enough real problems in my life, without entering into Sara Breed's grotesque world? Was I going to lie awake tonight in that silent house, imagining a circle of dark figures near the foot of that tall dead pine?

Go there, I decided. Go there right now. After all, I was dressed for it, in the old tan rain-or-shine coat I had bought while still in college. Perhaps, once I actually stood in that clearing, the thought of it would no longer disturb me. Instead it would seem to me a blessed spot, as it had that day when Mother and Sara had found me there after my long, sobbing search for the way home. And then Sara's dark fancies about the place would seem just that, fancies.

But what if I got lost, as I had when I was five? If only there was some way of marking my path as I went along. . . . Well, there was a way. It would make me feel rather a fool, but I would feel even more of a fool if I got lost.

About two miles outside Claverly a shopping mall sprawled beside the road. I stopped there and in the supermarket bought a box of cheap hard candy, each piece wrapped in either red or blue paper. Out in the parking lot I filled my coat pockets with the candy, dropped the flimsy paper box into a litter basket, and drove on.

About half a mile before I reached the small lake outside of Wessex, I turned to my left onto that much narrower dirt road. I followed it past the closed-for-the-season cottages, past the long stretch of woodland. Then I stopped the car in front of the boarded-up house where I had spent the first six years of my life.

I went through the gap where the fence gate had been and then walked around the house through the rain-wet weeds. One of the two crossed planks nailed over the back door was about to come loose, I noticed. I went on, past the ruins of a small shed. At the rear of the yard, too, the gate in the fence was missing. I went through the gap. Beyond was the wall of evergreens, mingled with oaks and maples just coming into leaf. There was a slight, almost undiscernible break in the undergrowth, which I knew must be the start of a path, in all probability the same one my errant five-year-old feet had taken that long-ago day.

It was pleasant in the woods, despite the dimming of the gray daylight, and despite the wet branches I had to

125

push aside. There was a smell of ferns and other green growing things, and there were lots of birds, filling the air with song as they courted or searched for nesting sites. A towhee accompanied me for a while, watching me from one sherry-colored eye as he flew along beside the path, pausing now and then to let me almost catch up with him and then flying ahead for a few yards.

Before long the path grew dim and then disappeared entirely. I hesitated for a moment. Then I went around a big oak tree. I dropped the first brightly wrapped piece of candy onto the thick leaf mold there and then went on in what I hoped was the same direction. Half an hour later I still had seen no sign of the little clearing. I was almost out of candy and, although my watch said it was only three o'clock, it seemed to me that the light had begun to fade. Then, just as I was about to turn back, I saw, through a break in the trees, the blasted pine with its jagged branches, a tall bleached shape among its still-living neighbors. I hurried forward, almost, but not quite, forgetting to drop two more pieces of candy.

The clearing seemed smaller than in my dim memory of it, but then, to a young child everything seems larger than it does to an adult. Across the clearing I could see the fairly well-defined entrance to another path, leading away in the opposite direction to the one by which I had come.

So apparently people did visit this spot. Many people. I looked around me for such signs as empty beer cans or crumpled cigarette wrappers. Nothing like that. Just spring-green grass, already quite long in this open space, and a few low bushes, and some tiny blue flowers whose name I didn't know.

Then, only inches from where I stood, I did see something lying in the grass, something that gleamed dully. I bent and picked it up. A candle stub, only about an inch and a half long. A black candle stub. Over there, a foot or so away, was another stub.

*Black* candles? Where on earth could anyone get black candles? Certainly I'd never seen any on sale. You'd have to make them yourself. But why would anyone—

I dropped the candle stub as if it had turned red-hot. It struck the toe of my shoe and caromed off to disappear in the grass. I'd just remembered what I'd heard about black candles. Black candles, black robes, black chalices. All of them were used in devil worship.

Could that be why people had brought black candles to this isolated spot? And not only on nights nearly eighteen years ago. Perhaps a week ago, or at most a few months. A bit of wax, lying here exposed to sun and rain, would soon grow dull and dirt encrusted, if it did not disintegrate entirely. That black stub had still had a sheen.

I thought of them, people deluded or depraved or both, meeting here in the dark. I thought of burning candles held below their hood-shadowed faces, faces that, if you could see them, would seem to waver in the candle's air-stirred glow. . . .

Like Peggy Crofton's face when I'd seen it through sluggishly moving cigarette smoke in that room off the ballroom. Like Jack Payson's face in the wavering light that came through the Bentley's rain-sheeted windshield.

Quite suddenly, fear descended upon me. An unreasoning fear of chic Peggy Crofton and her handsome cousin, and of my aloneness in this silent place, and of the hooded figures that, at least in my imagination, had stood not too long ago where I stood now.

I whirled around, darted out of the clearing. It is a wonder that, in my panic, I did not start off in the wrong direction, and thus miss the last of the candles I had dropped. But I saw both it and, a couple of yards beyond, the next to the last one.

There's an odd thing about panic. You seem to increase it just by the act of fleeing. Soon I began to have a sense of someone running silently behind me through the gray light. The feeling was so strong that I dared not look back, so strong that it was all I could do to keep following the trail I'd made for myself, rather than darting off into the woods and becoming thoroughly lost. Once I stumbled over a tree root or something and went down onto my hands and knees, certain that in another instant I would feel the grasp of that silent pursuer. Then I scrambled to my feet and ran on, despite the growing pain in my side.

For some unfathomable reason, I felt safer once I reached the path near the end of the woods. I even stopped and leaned against a tree trunk, breathing raggedly.

A new fear struck me then. The baby! But surely my panicky flight through the woods wouldn't do any harm, not when I was used to running. After a while, jogging now, I went on. When I finally emerged from the woods, I turned and looked back. No one. Just the path, paved with many years of autumn leaves, leading away through the trees. I went through the weedy yard of what had once been my mother's house and got into my car.

As I drove down the road past the empty summer cottages, I thought, "I've got to tell Guy." No matter what he might say, no matter how deranged he might think me, I could not bear alone the nightmarish vision that had sent me fleeing back through the woods.

But I wouldn't tell him in the house, that brand-new house that one might have thought ideal for a newly married couple, but that had meant little besides bad luck for us. Sometimes lately I'd had a sense that the house *listened*. Listened to my footsteps as I moved from room to room, listened to the voices of Diana Ross and Barry Manilow and Frank Sinatra pouring from a radio tuned loud.

On the shore of the little lake outside Wessex, there was a boathouse with a public phone booth beside it. I drove close to the booth and parked. On this gray day, there was no one around except the floating swans and some harsh-voiced sea gulls, visitors from the Long Island Sound a half-dozen miles away, who for some reason were circling above this freshwater lake.

I looked at my watch. Only four-forty-five. Still, Guy sometimes left his office early on Fridays. He might possibly be at the motel. Unless, I thought bleakly, he was staying somewhere else now, or unless he was out with someone, someone like Nicole. . . .

I went into the phone booth, looked up the motel's number, deposited a coin, dialed. A man's voice said, "I'll connect you with Mr. Nordeen's room."

Guy answered the phone so quickly that I got the feeling that he'd been hoping and waiting for a call. The question was, a call from whom?

"Hello, Guy. It's Linda."

"Linda!" The warmth in his voice made me feel weak with pleasure.

"Could I talk with you, Guy?"

"I'll be right over."

"No! I'm not at the house. I'm parked beside the boathouse at the lake. I'll wait for you here."

Anxiety came into his voice. "Is something wrong?"

"I'm not sick or hurt or anything like that. But please come as soon as you can."

Within fifteen minutes his rented convertible, its top down on this gray day, came to a stop beside me. Guy got out and then slid into the Mustang's front seat. "What is it, Linda?"

So as not to lose my courage, I began at once to tell him all of it. I spoke swiftly but disjointedly, sometimes doubling back to some bit of information I'd skipped. I told of Dilsey Wolsifer's strange coldness to me, and of her insistence that I was not going to be "happy" in Wessex. I spoke of how strange Peggy Crofton's face had looked through writhing cigarette smoke that afternoon when I returned to her house. I told him of Jack Payson's face, with features that seemed to waver and run together in the gray light coming through the rain-wet windshield. With my voice gathering speed, I told him of my second visit to Sara Breed, and of her story about that gathering in the woods.

Finally, although by then the look on Guy's face made my mouth feel so dry it was hard to speak, I told of my discovery of those candle ends and my panicky flight from the clearing.

I had expected to see incredulity in his face, and I did. But gradually his expression had turned to something much worse, a kind of sorrowful tenderness. His eyes said, as clearly as any words could have, "I should have realized it earlier. There's something wrong with you. You're sick, my darling."

At last I stopped talking and just looked at him, silently pleading for his belief. He said gently, "You know I've no use for Jack Payson. And even though I do like Peggy, I realize no one would ever choose her to play Elsie Dinsmore. But the very idea of one or both of them belonging to some kind of—what the hell do they call it?"

"A coven," I managed to say. "I think it's called a coven."

"Whatever it's called, the very thought of them meeting in the woods at night to practice some sort of mumbo jumbo—"

He paused for a moment, and then went on, "Now listen to me, Linda. In the first place, there is no such thing as a witch. There are just people who think they can gain supernatural power through certain practices, or at least hope they can. But at least in this day and age such people are usually thrill-seeking teenagers, not mature, well-established citizens of a highly conservative town like Wessex. Can't you see that, darling, can't you?"

"But Sara Breed saw—"

"Linda! Sara Breed is insane. How can you take seriously anything she tells you?"

"The candles," I said, wretchedly but stubbornly. "I held the stub of a black candle, right in my hand."

For a moment I thought he was going to say, "You *think* you held a candle." Instead he said, "All right, I'm sure there are other explanations for that candle, but let's try this one on for size. Let's suppose that a bunch of teenagers met up there last Halloween, say. Didn't you

131

tell me you saw a path leading away from the opposite side of the clearing?"

I nodded.

"Well, if you'd followed it you probably would have come out after a couple of miles at an abandoned quarry. The road isn't used now except as a lovers' lane. Some kids could have left their cars at the quarry last Halloween and then climbed to that clearing, taking with them whatever paraphernalia they had—"

His voice trailed off. Was it only that, I wondered, a kids' prank? I tried to visualize teenagers standing in a circle, some of them giggling, others saying, "Come on, you guys! Get serious. No point in coming up here if you're just going to fool around."

The idea didn't ring true for me. It wasn't prankish teenagers whose presence I had sensed as I stood in that clearing. Evil people, coldly serious people, had been meeting there for a long time, long enough that their aura remained there in their absence.

Guy had been watching my face. He said, "Don't you see, darling?"

I shook my head.

He reached out and stroked my hair. "We'd better see someone, dearest, and then we'll go away from here—"

"See someone? You mean a psychiatrist?"

"Yes, Linda."

"Guy, I'm not crazy!"

"I didn't say you were. But any of us, if subjected to enough strain—"

Something in my face must have stopped him, because he broke off and then said with a rush, "All right. The first thing we'll do is to leave this town. We'll live in New York. I shouldn't have any trouble joining a New York importing firm. And if I do, I can go into another line of business."

I thought of Guy in New York, away not only from his hometown but from the firm that had been his family's for generations. And all because of a wife he believed to be not right in the head.

"No," I said.

"Darling, it's not just the two of us now. There's the baby to think of."

"I am thinking of the baby."

What kind of parents would we be—a father not only self-exiled but convinced that his wife was mentally ill, and a mother wavering between self-doubt and a stubborn belief that, back there in Wessex, she had been the target of some viciously inimical force.

I had hoped that he would believe me and try to help me. But since he either could not or would not, I would have to try to help myself. I had a sense of loneliness almost as palpable as if a sudden icy wind had swept off the lake to wrap itself around me.

"Let's go home, darling," Guy said, "right now."

Home. That house. Within minutes after we entered it, we probably would be saying harsh and hateful things to each other.

"No, Guy. I want to be alone to—to think over the things you've said."

Hope mingled with the worry in his face. "If you do, Linda, I think you'll realize I'm right. You've just been subjected to too many strains. Coming back to this place where that awful thing happened to your mother, and you and I not getting along too well sometimes, and then your idea about Nicole and me. And of course there's the baby. I've heard that pregnant women get odd notions.

So think about it, darling. Think hard. And then we'll decide what we should do."

The anxiety in his voice sharpened. "But I hate the idea of your being alone there, even for one more night."

"I'll be all right. Guy, there's something else. You've been seeing Nicole, haven't you?"

"I've seen her once. She called me at the motel last Sunday and we went for a drive. But darling, for God's sake don't start worrying about that again. I'm not in love with Nicole. It's you I love."

He didn't have to assure me of that. Not now. If he hadn't loved me, loved me a lot, the belief that I was mentally unstable would have brought some measure of repulsion into his eyes. Instead I had seen nothing there but shock, followed by a concerned tenderness.

"I know," I said. "It's just that I saw you with her. Neither of you saw me. I'd twisted my ankle slightly and was resting beside the road through that new subdivision. Nicole was crying."

He nodded. "Over Jean-Paul. She has reason to think he's planning to marry someone else. I tried to tell her that a couple of years from now she'd be wondering what she ever saw in him, but I couldn't convince her of that. It's a father complex, I guess. I can't think why else a girl like Nicole would want to marry a phony French count twice her age. But it's nothing for you to be concerned about, darling."

"I know," I said again. "I—I think you'd better go now."

He took my face in his hands and kissed me. It was a prolonged kiss but very gentle. "Okay if I telephone you tomorrow? Or would you rather I waited until you call me? I mean, I don't want to interfere with your thinking about—"

"I'd rather you waited."

There was a struggle in his face. I could see he was wondering if it wouldn't be best to take me, by force if necessary, to the nearest source of medical help. I braced myself. But the look faded from his eyes. He said, "All right, darling. If you want to call me tomorrow, I may be at my office. I figured I'd catch up on some work then, even though it'll be Saturday."

Was it because of piled-up work, I wondered, that he was going to his office, or was he just trying to escape from his own worried thoughts? He said, "I'll hope to see you very soon, darling," and got out of the car.

When he had driven away I sat there for a while, staring at the wind-ruffled water. There was one person in this town who might be able to help me, if only she would. Dilsey Wolsifer. Dilsey had known both my mother and Sara Breed. If she chose, she might be able to tell me whether or not there was any basis in fact for Sara's story that evil people had ordered her to lead my mother to that moonlit pool. She might be able to tell me, also, if there was any validity in the feeling I'd had ever since I returned to Wessex, a feeling that the very air around me held some hidden menace.

I looked at my watch. Eighteen minutes past five. But the bakery kept open until five-thirty. And even if it closed before I got there, I could still see her. She had an apartment above the bakery, at the end of a flight of stairs leading up from the street.

The bakery was still open when I slid my car into a Main Street parking space. But the woman behind the counter was not Dilsey Wolsifer. Thin and blond and around fifty, she gave me a we're-about-to-close look.

"Help you?"

"I wanted to see Miss Wolsifer."

135

"She's sick. Anything I can do for you?"

"Could I go up and see her? She's upstairs, isn't she?"

"Yes, but you can't see her. No one can for a few days. Doctor's orders."

I said, alarmed, "Then it's serious?"

"A minor heart seizure, the doctor says. But if she doesn't get complete rest for a while she might have a bad one."

For a few moments I stood in silent dismay. Then I asked, "Are you a relative of Miss Wolsifer's?"

"No, I just help out here now and then." She paused. "You're Mrs. Nordeen, aren't you?"

"Yes."

"Pleased to meet you. I'm Mrs. Schroeder. Now I don't want to seem rude, Mrs. Nordeen, but if you're not going to buy anything I'd like to close."

I looked at the counter display and pointed at the first tray my gaze lighted upon. "A half dozen of those chocolate cookies, please."

She put the cookies in a box, tied a string around it. As soon as I stepped out onto the sidewalk I heard her locking the door. I got into my car and sat there for a few minutes, looking at the people who moved along the sidewalk through the fading light. But in my mind's eye I was seeing my great-grandmother's headstone: "Born Humility, Mass., 1879."

Humility, a town that, according to the Presbyterian minister, probably no longer even existed. But some knowledge of it existed in Dilsey Wolsifer's mind, something that had caused alarm to leap into her face when I questioned her about it.

Even if the town no longer existed, the site of it did. And there would be people around, people on farms or in towns that went on existing after Humility disappeared.

The filling station at the end of Main Street would still be open. I could buy a Massachusetts road map there and make sure that no such place existed now. Then tomorrow morning I could telephone the Massachusetts Historical Society. Surely there was such a group, probably with headquarters in Boston. Every state had a historical society. And they, if anyone, would know where that vanished town had been.

Even if I found the place, there was little likelihood that it would tell me anything. But since I could think of nothing else to do, I'd go up there.

I backed the Mustang into the street and turned toward the filling station.

EVEN BEFORE I had breakfast the next morning, I
called Boston Information on the bedroom phone, asked
for the Massachusetts Historical Society's number and
wrote it down. Then, wearing a blue cotton robe over my
nightgown, I descended to a kitchen filled with silence
broken only by the refrigerator's hum. I made toast and
tea and sat down with it in the breakfast nook. Through
the window I could see drops of dew on the rear lawn,
gleaming like prisms in the early sunlight. At least I
would have good weather for my drive north.

After I'd finished my tea and toast I glanced at my
watch. Three minutes of nine. The Historical Society's
office might be opening soon. I climbed to my bedroom
and dialed that Boston phone number.

After the phone had rung five times, a testy-sounding
male voice said, "Historical Society."

"Good morning. I'm calling from Connecticut to see if
you could give me any information at all about a Massachusetts town called Humility."

"Humility! I never heard of it. Where is it?"

"As far as I know, it isn't anywhere now. I mean, everyone must have left it, for some reason or other. But
maybe you have a record of where it used to be."

"Madame, you had better call back on Monday. On Saturdays I'm the only person here."

"Please, it's quite urgent." I felt it was. How much longer could I live with my unresolved tensions, my shadowy fears? "Maybe you have some information about the town on your computer."

After a moment he said, in a reluctant voice, "Well, hold on. I'll see."

I waited, visualizing him as an irritable little man, annoyed with me for interrupting his reading, or crossword puzzle solving, or whatever other diversions he enjoyed on quiet Saturday mornings. Finally he came back to the phone. "Yes, there's a mention of such a town in the correspondence of Governor Phelps of Massachusetts. He was a late seventeenth-century governor, an appointee of the British Crown, of course. In 1693 he wrote to a friend that he had received a communication from some families who—I'll give you the exact quote—'did depart ye town of Salem ten months since for another place, which they did call Humility.'"

"That's all? He didn't say where this town was?"

"I gave you the entire quote. There may be additional pertinent information stored in the computer. Call back Monday, when someone more expert than I will be able to help you."

"Please! Don't hang up." A date learned in a high school American History class had flashed into my mind. "Did you say that this governor—"

"Phelps, Governor Phelps."

"Did you say that this quote of his you gave me was dated 1693?"

"That's what I said."

"And he referred to people leaving Salem ten months earlier?"

139

"Yes. Now if you'll call back—"

"More than likely, that means they left Salem in 1692." I paused. "When were the Salem witchcraft trials?"

He was silent for several seconds. Then he said, "You're right! You're absolutely right. The trials were in 1692."

No boredom in his voice now. But then, I've noticed that people seem to take a perverse pride in the more disgraceful episodes in their local history. San Franciscans romanticize the Barbary Coast days. Missourians like to talk about the James brothers and their fellow outlaws. And at least some Massachusetts people, I was learning, relish the thought of those trials that ended with nineteen people dangling from gallows and one dead beneath the weights that had been heaped on his bound body.

"Hold on again," he said. "I'm sure I can get you more information about people who left Salem around that time."

He did. Records of the Congregational Church in Salem revealed that at the time of the witchcraft trials "divers persons did depart this place to seek new habitations in ye western part of ye colony." And the diary of a seventeenth-century Massachusetts woman yielded another place name. In 1698 she recorded that a couple who "did flee this place" in 1692 had returned from a settlement "yclept Havers Falls."

"And Havers Falls *is* still in existence," the animated voice at the other end of the line said. "I looked it up in an atlas before I came back to the phone. It's up near the Vermont border, about thirty miles west of Greenfield. It seems to me logical that Humility might have been near Havers Falls. I mean, if all these people fled Salem at approximately the same time, they might have settled near each other."

"I think so too."

"You're going to try to find this place?"

"Yes."

"Do you mind telling me why you're so interested in the matter?"

"My great-grandmother and my grandmother were both born there."

"I see. Well, if you find out anything more about the place—why the town disappeared, for instance—will you let me know? My name is Feversham, David Feversham."

"Yes, I'll let you know. And thank you very much indeed, Mr. Feversham."

I sat for a moment, my hand resting on the phone. Then I got up and changed my robe and nightgown for jeans, a yellow turtleneck sweater, and my rain-or-shine coat.

As always, the traffic congestion in Hartford was appalling. I drove with tense care, trying to be sure that I did not make the wrong turns, and trying not to think of Guy, even though, when highway Ninety-one led me over a viaduct, I could actually see the tall building where Nordeen Importers had its main office. He'd probably be working this Saturday, Guy had said. How I longed to take the next right turn off the highway and go to him. But, much as we loved each other, Guy could not help me, not as long as he believed I was threatened only by phantoms of my own imagination.

Once I was through Hartford, the highway took me straight north toward the Massachusetts border. Under other circumstances, I would have enjoyed that drive. The traffic wasn't too bad, in spite of those gigantic trailer trucks that, klaxons blaring, rocketed past me at illegal speeds. The countryside was lovely in its fresh spring green. The highway kept crossing back and forth over the broad Connecticut River, sparkling in the sun. And in stretches of woodland, white dogwood blossoms gave the impression of snow falling among the newly leaved oaks and maples.

North of Greenfield, Massachusetts, I turned, pulse

142

quickening, onto a state road. According to the road map, Havers Falls (population 1250) was only about thirty miles away.

It took me the better part of an hour to get there. After a few miles, the state road became potholed, and the narrow county road onto which I turned was in even worse shape. Plainly not much tax money was spent on this sparsely populated part of Massachusetts. But finally I did reach Havers Falls.

Such a sad little town. It seemed to consist mainly of one street straggling along the hillside above a rushing river. At least half the business establishments, including a movie theater, stood empty. A hundred yards or so short of the falls, which, I suppose, gave the town its name, a bridge led across the river to a grim-looking building that must once have been some sort of factory, probably a textile mill. Whatever it once had been, it stood deserted now, some of its windows broken, others boarded over. In another fifty years, I reflected, Havers Falls might vanish almost as completely as Humility had—except, of course, for that prisonlike brick building. It probably would go on standing there until someone had it pulled down.

A few doors beyond the boarded-up movie house was a small restaurant, with the words "Eddie's Place" in white letters on the plate-glass window. I parked my car and went in. The girl behind the counter was about eighteen, with thin blond hair that looked as if it needed a shampoo. I sat down on one of the stools, ordered coffee, and then asked, "Have you ever heard of a town named Humility around here? I mean, it used to be around here."

She set a thick white cup and saucer in front of me. "Humility! You must be kidding."

143

"No. I'm fairly certain it was around here someplace. But it may have lost all its population by—oh, maybe 1890."

"Before my time."

Because of my tense nerves I was tempted to retort, "So was the Battle of Bunker Hill, but I presume you've heard of it." Instead I asked, "Can you think of anyone in town who might have heard of the place?"

"Not offhand. But say! There're some people about five miles out of town who might be able to tell you something. The Canfields. They used to be farmers. But now they've got a couple of gas pumps, and in the summer they sell vegetables that Mr. Canfield raises in a little bitty old truck garden. Mrs. Canfield told me once that her people have been in this part of Massachusetts for about three hundred years."

"Thank you," I said. I paid her and left.

I found the Canfields' roadside place without any trouble. A woman of about sixty, gray hair drawn back into a neat bun, sat in a straight wooden chair near the gas pumps with a magazine in her hands. As I drove in, she stood up and laid the magazine on the chair seat. I asked her to fill the tank. After I'd paid her I asked, "Are you Mrs. Canfield?"

"That's right." Her brown eyes were friendly behind rimless glasses.

"A girl in a restaurant in Havers Falls gave me your name. She said you might be able to help me. You see, I'm looking for the place where a certain town used to be. Its name was Humility?"

"My heavens! It's been years since I've heard anyone mention Humility."

My heart leaped. "Then you know something about it?"

144

"Oh, sure. My grandmother told me about it. She could remember when there were people there. Only a couple of hundred or so. It was never much of a town. Then sometime in the 1890s there was a typhoid epidemic. It wasn't the first one to hit Humility, not by a long shot. Maybe there was always something wrong with the wells up there, my grandmother said. Anyway, the last epidemic finished the town. More than half the people died, and the ones who didn't just packed up and left."

Including my great-grandmother, a young widow named Charity Tolan, who with her two-year-old daughter had somehow made her way to Wessex, that handsome village on the Connecticut River.

"I used to play up there with other kids when I was little," Mrs. Canfield said. "We still had our farm then." She threw a wistful look at a wooden stand, which displayed a few bunches of radishes and spring onions. "But as I was saying, we kids would play up there. That was back in the 1930s, and the buildings were all long since gone. Some had burned down because of lightning, or of tramps building fires to cook on. Others were pulled to pieces by folks who needed siding or flooring or roof shingles. But there was still stuff up there to interest kids. Bits of colored glass inside the foundation of what had been the church, and old bent spoons and bits of crockery. Once I found half of a wooden soldier. But that was around fifty years ago. I doubt that there's anything up there now, except the graveyard, of course."

"There's a graveyard?"

"Oh, sure. A few graves date back almost three hundred years, to the late 1600s. The oldest headstones are more or less sunken and some of them are missing, although it's hard for me to imagine them getting stolen. On the whole, folks around here are pretty nice." She paused. "You've got some special interest in the place?"

"Yes. I learned recently that my great-grandmother was born in Humility. So was her daughter, my grandmother."

"Were they, now! Well, if you want to look at the graveyard, you won't have any trouble finding it. It has an old stone wall around it."

"How do I—"

"Just keep on this road for about half a mile. Then turn right onto this narrow dirt road. It's really more of a track than a road. Leads to a couple of farms way back in the hills. But you'll get to the place you want long before that. I'd say that old graveyard is only about two miles from where you turn off this road."

THE ROAD that was "really more of a track" was poor indeed, narrow and deeply rutted. It led over gently rolling country that perhaps once had been farmland, but was now bare except for tall wild grass and bushes and an occasional oak tree.

Vanished Humility had occupied a hilltop. I stopped the car beside the little graveyard and got out. Wind whispered through the grass. High above me, some bird, perhaps a meadowlark, spilled a song down through the early afternoon air. Otherwise the place was silent.

If I had not known there had once been a town here, I might never have noticed the few traces that were left. The cemetery's crumbling low wall was partly obscured by bushes. Only slight depressions in the grassy earth marked where old houses had stood above their shallow cellars. The stone foundation of one fairly large rectangular building, undoubtedly the church's, was still visible, but like the cemetery wall it was partly obscured by grass and vines and low bushes. I thought suddenly of the Black Death, and how it had wiped out whole villages in medieval England, leaving no sign that generations of men and women had worked and loved and struggled there.

I went through a gap in the cemetery wall where once

a gate must have been. Immediately I realized that this was the most recently used part of the cemetery, the area where the typhoid victims were buried. There were forty or more headstones, all dated 1899. Just beyond those graves I found what I knew must be my great-grand-father's headstone. John Tolan, "husband of Charity Tolan," had died at the age of forty-five in 1898. Thus he had been dead only a year when his widow left this ty-phoid-stricken place, taking with her the tiny daughter who grew up to become my grandmother.

Why had my great-grandmother brought her child to Wessex? That was something I might never know.

As I moved farther back in the cemetery, the head-stones grew smaller and their inscriptions harder to read. Some were so badly worn that they were illegible. Other stones had sunk so deeply into the earth that only the top one or two lines of their inscriptions were visible. Near the wall opposite the gate, almost three hundred years of sun and snow and rain had worn many headstones smooth.

I could read only one marker dating from Humility's earliest days. In 1697 or 1699—the figures were too worn for me to be sure—a woman named Charity Haleworthy had died at the age of eighty-six. As I read that headstone, a shiver went through me. Although the stone did not say so, this long-dead woman, with the same given name as my mother, almost certainly had been among those who fled the Salem witch hunters.

I turned around then. Scrutinizing the headstones more carefully as I went, I moved slowly back toward the cem-etery entrance. A Charity Hewlett had died in 1735, a Charity Barnes in 1772, a Charity Chadwick in 1808. All in all, in the more than two hundred years of Humility's existence, seven women with the given name of Charity had been buried in this graveyard.

I walked out of the cemetery and sat down on its stone wall. My heartbeats felt faint and rapid, and I could hear an odd humming in my ears. Had the women of my family, descendants of that Charity Haleworthy who had fled Salem, passed down through the generations more than a first name? Passed something evil and ancient down to my mother and to me?

No! My mother had not been evil. *I* was not evil.

There in the silence of that long-deserted place, I forced myself to remember what little I had heard or read about witchcraft.

Unless my recollections were incorrect, witchcraft had been part of the "Old Religion," the pagan belief that flourished in one form or another all over the world before it was conquered and outlawed by Christianity.

The men and women priests of the Old Religion had been called witches, a term which, like the word *wit*, came from an ancient root word meaning "to know." Thus witches were "wise people," possessed of the knowledge of magical rites. If I remembered correctly, it was believed that the power gained through practicing those rites could be used for either evil or good, to harm or to protect, to sicken or to heal. Evil practitioners, or black witches, acknowledged Satan as their lord. White witches revered the Earth Goddess, that ancient deity to whom people still pay unthinking honor when they use the term "Mother Nature."

I thought of my mother emerging from the woods to enter our yard, the sun on her blond hair, a little smile on her lips, and a small basket filled with wild plants on one arm. I thought of how she would stand at the sinkboard in

149

our old house, making little bundles of green things to take down to Dilsey's small grocery store, where people would buy them for various purposes—to make salads, or to flavor soups, or to brew an invigorating but caffeine-free tea.

No, if there was such a thing as witchcraft, and my mother had practiced it, she had not done so for evil purposes.

Dilsey Wolsifer, I thought desperately. If I could just see her. Probably she was the only person alive who perhaps both could and would give me the information I needed. And yet days might pass before she would physically be able to see me. Days when I would just have to wait in that silent house. And even if she recovered completely, she still might refuse to talk to me.

But there was a chance, just a chance, that I might be able to talk to her much sooner, maybe only a few hours from now. At least it was worth a try. I looked at my watch. A quarter of two. If I hurried, I could make the drive back to Wessex in less than three hours. And the bakery, like a number of village businesses, stayed open until seven on Saturday nights.

I stood up and turned around. I took one last look at where they lay, those ancestors of mine, stretching back to a time when followers of the Old Religion were often hanged or burned or pressed to death under heavy weights in accordance with the Biblical injunction; "Thou shalt not suffer a witch to live."

How many of them had held secretly to the ancient faith, even though they also did homage to the Christian God each Sunday in that church whose crumbling foundation I could see through tangled vines and wild grass?

I got into my car and drove down the rutted road.

150

IT WAS not yet five o'clock when I slid the Mustang into a parking space a few yards from the bakery's entrance. I'd made excellent time, stopping only once for a hastily eaten cheese sandwich at a McDonald's near Springfield, and getting through the Hartford traffic before the worst of the rush hour.

The same thin blond woman was behind the bakery counter. To my hopeful surprise, her face lit up at sight of me. I said, "Hello, Mrs. Schroeder. Is Miss Wolsifer better today?"

"No, I'm afraid not. You can see her, though. In fact, she very much wants to see you."

I said, vastly grateful but a little incredulous, "Yesterday you told me—"

"I was following her doctor's orders. But when I told her a little before noon today that you'd been here, she insisted that I phone you. There was no answer, but I promised her I would keep trying until I did get in touch with you."

"Does her doctor—"

"Yes, he knows about it. He said that it would be better for her to see you than to keep fretting over not seeing

151

you. You can just go up the stairs. Her apartment door is unlocked."

I thanked her. Then, heartbeats fast, I went out onto the sidewalk and climbed narrow stairs with linoleum-covered risers. I opened the unlocked door at the top and went in. Her living-room windows faced east, and so even though it was only late afternoon, the light in there was somewhat dim. I could make out, though, that the room was filled with worn but comfortable-looking furniture, including a dark blue overstuffed sofa, a matching arm-chair, and a tan rug. Then, as I moved toward an open doorway that I thought must lead to the bedroom, I saw something else, something that stopped me in my tracks.

Between the windows stood a small pie-crust table, its top crowded with photographs. Among the pictures of people I did not know there was a framed snapshot of my mother, looking much as in my last memories of her. In the picture, she sat on the porch step of that old house, smiling up at the camera, and holding on her lap a little girl of about two, undoubtedly myself. In another snapshot she sat at a table with an older woman whose face seemed familiar to me. My grandmother? Yes, it must have been.

There was also a snapshot of me at the age of five or six, squinting into the sun and holding by one arm a doll with dark curls. Although I had no idea of what had become of that doll, I could remember her name. I'd called her Jackie, after President Kennedy's beautiful widow.

So Dilsey's unfriendliness toward me had been just pretense, I thought, feeling puzzled but thankful. Otherwise she would not have kept that old snapshot of me.

I walked to that open doorway, tapped very lightly on its frame and then looked into the room. As I did so, Dilsey opened her eyes. She lay in bed, worn hands clasped on the green rayon bedspread, gray braids framing her lined face.

I said, "Oh, forgive me! I didn't know you were asleep."

"I wasn't." Her voice sounded both weak and hoarse. "Come in, Linda. Sit down."

I took the straight chair beside the bed. Now that I was close to her, she appeared ill indeed, her face pallid and with brownish circles under the eyes. And yet, paradoxically, she seemed to me to look younger, more like the Dilsey of my childhood memories. Perhaps that was because of a softness in her eyes that hadn't been there the last two times I'd seen her.

I said tentatively, "Are you sure that you're strong enough—"

"It doesn't matter." Dryness in her tone now. "I don't need strength just to lie in bed. And I don't think I'm ever going to get up again."

"Oh, please don't say—"

"Don't argue with me, child. It just wastes time and energy, and I've got things to tell you. Things I *must* tell you, since you didn't take my advice to leave this town."

I waited, hands clenched in my lap. She said, "You once asked me about a town in Massachusetts called Humility." She broke off, looking not at me but the ceiling.

After a few seconds, unable to bear her silence, I said, "I drove up there today, to where the town used to be."

Her gaze turned to my face. "Why? Why did you go there?"

"It was because of things that happened yesterday."

Swiftly I told her of my second conversation with Sara Breed in that state hospital visiting room. I told of how

153

I'd gone to that clearing and found the candle stubs and then fled in panic.

"I—I tried to talk to my husband about it, but he thought that I was just—just—"

"Imagining things?" Again her voice was dry.

"Yes. And so I came here to talk to you."

"But Mrs. Schroeder turned you away."

I nodded. "I just sat in my car out front for a while, thinking about the sort of scared look that came into your face the day I mentioned the headstones of my grandmother's and great-grandmother's in the Presbyterian churchyard. I thought of how you'd denied knowing where Humility was. And then I decided to try to find the place, in the hope that just seeing it might tell me something, anything at all."

I spoke of my phone conversation with the man at the Massachusetts Historical Society and then my drive north to that little hilltop graveyard.

I stopped speaking. Silence settled down. Then Dilsey said, "It's plain you've already guessed a lot of the truth. Still, there are things you need to know. The trouble is, I don't know where to begin. . . ."

Her tired voice trailed off. After a moment I said, "Maybe you could tell me how you came to know my mother, and my grandmother—"

"And your great-grandmother. All right. I was about fourteen when I met your great-grandmother and your grandmother. My parents and I were newcomers to Wessex then."

"Where had you come from?"

"A little town in New Hampshire. My father had the dry cleaning shop there. It had never made much money, and so when he was notified that this bachelor uncle of

154

his had left him a grocery store in Wessex, he sold his cleaning business and brought my mother and me down here. We'd been here only about a week when your great-grandmother and her daughter walked into the grocery one day."

"You say you were fourteen?"

"Yes. I guess your great-grandmother was about fifty or a little younger at that time. Your grandmother was in her twenties, although of course she wasn't your grandmother then. She wasn't even married."

I thought of those two ancestresses of mine walking into that grocery store. The year, I calculated swiftly, must have been around 1930 or a little earlier. Had they worn loose, long-waisted dresses, and cloche hats that came down almost to their eyebrows? Perhaps on one of the shelves there'd been a radio, one of those big ones with a pointed top and coarsely woven cloth over the speaker, playing a Rudy Vallée number.

Dilsey said, "I recognized what they were as soon as I saw them. So did my mother. Followers of the Old Belief always recognize each other."

Stomach tightening into a knot, I thought of the strange aspect in which I had once seen Jack Payson's face, and later Peggy Crofton's. Had I recognized something in them that was invisible to ordinary people?

Dilsey was saying, "A few years later, your grandmother got married and gave birth to a little girl, your mother. I was still in my teens, but just the same I felt very close to your grandmother. And as your mother grew up I felt very close to *her*. When you were born, I helped your mother with her housework for a week after she brought you home from the hospital. And that very bad year—the year when she lost both your father and

155

your grandmother—I stayed with her for days at a time. You weren't even three years old then."

She fell silent. I said, "And you came to take care of me that terrible morning after my mother had been found."

"Yes. I brought you here, to this apartment, until those cousins of your father's came to take you to New York with them. I loved you, but I was glad to see you go."

Even though I was almost sure I knew the answer to that, I asked, "Why?"

"Because *she* was here by then. Peggy Crofton. That poor rich fool Hal Crofton had married her up in Mansfield and brought her to Wessex. I wondered if he ever realized that it had been like introducing a deadly plague into this town. Maybe he did realize it. Maybe she taunted him with it, finally. That might have been why he shot himself."

I said, in a voice that sounded strange even to my own ears, "Then she's—she's a—"

Dilsey nodded. "Yes, a black witch, a very evil and clever and powerful one. And hate-filled, of course. Only those filled with hate could use their special powers the way she has. What caused her to be like that I have no idea. Perhaps something that happened when she was very young. All I'm sure of is that the hatred is there."

She fell silent for a few moments, gaze again fixed on the ceiling. Then she said, "And having so much money has made her all the more powerful. Even women of the oldest families in Wessex not only accepted her but competed for invitations to Hal Crofton's mansion. Soon Peggy was running this town. And although ordinary people didn't notice it, bad things happened to people who crossed her in even minor ways. Billy Barstein, who directed traffic in the summer back in those days, was foolish enough to give her a traffic ticket, despite the fuss

156

she made. The next day he fell down the Town Hall steps and broke his leg in two places. The bone didn't knit properly, and so he had to retire from the force. And then there was a woman named May Turnbull who objected to Peggy being named to the board of trustees of the Wessex Art Association. Probably it was only because Mrs. Turnbull was one of those people who object to almost everybody and everything. But anyway, Mrs. Turnbull had a dizzy spell soon after that and ran her car into a tree. She didn't go to an Art Association meeting or any other kind from then on, because she was confined to a wheelchair the rest of her life. There were quite a few incidents like that."

My mouth felt dry. I said, "Did my mother—"

"Try to fight her? Yes. Maybe you don't remember, Linda, but your mother was the sort who liked nearly everybody. She liked poor Billy Barstein, and crabby Mrs. Turnbull, and she especially liked Danny Eggerton."

"Who was—"

"Danny was a delivery boy for several stores in town. The summer he was thirteen, Peggy closed up her house and went to Switzerland for several months. Danny and another boy sneaked onto the Crofton grounds to play ball and accidentally broke a big hole in the greenhouse where Peggy raised her prize Bird of Paradise flowers. When she got home, she soon found out who did it. Danny never played ball again because he went blind. Nobody could find out why. He just went blind."

I made an inarticulate sound.

"It was because of Danny," Dilsey said, "that your mother finally decided to fight. I begged her not to. Peggy had grown very powerful by then. She had gotten a coven together. Do you know what that is, Linda?"

"I—I think so. It's a certain number of—"

157

"Thirteen. I don't know how serious the other coven members were. I imagine most were just bored women looking for thrills. Perhaps some were so socially ambitious they were ready to do almost anything Peggy Crofton suggested. Perhaps one or two were as serious as Peggy herself. But it didn't matter how strong their commitment was. They still increased her power."

She stopped speaking, coughed weakly and pressed one hand to her chest. I said, "Maybe you'd better stop—"

"Be quiet, Linda. I have to tell these things. You see, a witch can exercise certain powers without the aid of a coven. My mother and I were never part of a coven, nor was your mother or grandmother. But forming a coven can increase a witch's power many times over. And Peggy had her coven. Just as poor Sara Breed told you, they met up in that clearing, and still do.

"But despite all I could say, your mother was determined to fight Peggy. She even went to Peggy and threatened to try to convince everyone of the truth about her, although betraying a witch, whether black or white, to unbelievers is a crime against the Earth Mother herself."

Dilsey stopped speaking. I managed to say, "You're telling me that that was why—why my mother died?"

She nodded. "I never knew until today why Peggy chose to use that poor, dim-witted Sara Breed. But now that you've told me about your conversation with Sara, I think I see why. Peggy and the others wanted to punish her for spying. Maybe, too, they wanted to experiment a little, wanted to see if they could make that poor retarded woman entirely their creature. . . ."

Her voice trailed off. I said, dry mouthed, "Do you think they hypnotized her?"

"To judge by what Sara told you, I'd say yes. She said

158

she went to sleep up there, and when she woke up she was alone in the clearing. But after that there were voices in her head, threatening her, telling her what to do. There's a term for that, I think."

"Post-hypnotic suggestion?"

"Yes."

"I'm not sure," I said, "but I think I've heard that it's hard to hypnotize people of low intelligence."

"Perhaps it would be hard for ordinary hypnotists, but we're not talking about ordinary people. And perhaps Sara's being retarded was part of the challenge."

We were both silent for about a minute. I could hear automobile horns down in the street, and a young girl's voice rising up from the sidewalk: " . . . gross, utterly *gross*. And yet she thinks she's Brooke Shields or somebody."

Dilsey said, "I've never been brave, like your mother. And of course, I was a good deal older than she had been. After the Cartwrights took you away, I did my best not to arouse Peggy Crofton's enmity. I even sold off my stock in the grocery store and opened a bakery, as a sign to her that I wasn't even going to sell the sort of medicinal herbs that your mother used to collect in the woods. I've been completely—well, maybe immobilized is the word. Then I heard that Guy Nordeen had married Charity Edwards's daughter and was bringing her back here. I knew that would reawaken Peggy's antagonism not only to your mother but also to me, who'd been your mother's friend."

She went on, "But it wasn't just on my own account that I didn't want you to remain here. I was afraid of what Peggy might do to Charity Edwards's daughter. True, she might assume that you'd been raised with no

159

knowledge of your—your heritage. But she couldn't be sure that you would not gain such knowledge somehow and turn into the same sort of thorn in her side that your mother had been. And so I was sure that, at the very least, she'd try to get rid of you, using methods that might be very unpleasant.

"I tried to warn you, tried to get you to persuade your husband to leave this town. But I was too afraid of Peggy Crofton to tell you my reasons. Well, I'm not afraid of her now. I know now that I'm not going to last much longer, no matter what I do or don't do." She paused. "*Have* unpleasant things been happening to you?"

I said reluctantly, "Yes." I told her of the depression that seemed to be in the very air of that brand-new house, and of its odd, dead silence, and the way Guy and I got on each other's nerves whenever we were within its walls. I spoke too of the appalling mistake I had made with the brass cleaner.

She said matter-of-factly, "Peggy must have prepared the place for you before you even set foot in it."

"Prepared?"

"There are certain things—certain powders, for instance—which can alter the atmosphere of a house. She must have put some of them in your house. Or perhaps she had Jack Payson do it."

Again I thought of his grotesquely altered face in the wavering gray light that came through the rain-sheeted windshield. I felt the hairs rise on my forearms. "Then Jack Payson is—"

"A warlock. He came down here from Boston several years ago. I'm sure Peggy had sent for him. Now will you do as I say, Linda? Will you leave this place? Persuade your husband to go with you if you can. If you can't, leave without him."

160

When I didn't answer she said, in a flat voice, "What is it? Don't you believe what I've been telling you?"

I said wretchedly, "Forgive me, but I'm just not sure. Oh, I'm certain you wouldn't consciously mislead me, but still—"

"Still, I could be just a crazy old woman. Is that it?"

"Oh, please! I only meant that I need some time to think about the things you've said."

"It's all right, child. I'm not angry. But I've done all I can to help you." She sounded very old and very tired. "The rest is up to you."

It was a dismissal. I had a bleak sense of my aloneness. "Could I ask just one more question?"

"All right."

"Why did my great-grandmother come to Wessex?"

"Oh, that. That was pure happenstance. After she left Humility, she had to make a living for herself and her baby, and so she went down to Springfield, walking a lot of the way."

I pictured that young woman back there at the turn of the century, trudging along the dusty highway with her little girl in her arms.

"In Springfield, a family hired her to cook for them. A spinster from Wessex happened to be visiting that particular household. She took such a liking to your great-grandmother that she offered her better wages to work for her."

"In Wessex?"

"Yes. When the woman died about ten years later, she left her house and what income she had to your great-grandmother. Later the house passed to your grandmother and then to your mother."

"So it was the house I was born in."

"Yes."

"Thank you for telling me. Thank you for everything, Dilsey. I appreciate what you're trying to do for me more than I could possibly say. But I do have to think things over before I come to a decision. I have to."

"All right, child." Although the deeply circled eyes looked sad and worried, she managed to smile at me for the first time since I had come into the room. "I can understand that. But please go now. I'm very, very tired."

## TWENTY-FOUR

I WENT DOWN to my car. Near sunset light filled the street now. I sat behind the wheel of the Mustang and looked through the windshield at people passing along the sidewalk. A red-haired teenage boy in jeans and a Greek fisherman's sweater, pressing a transistor radio to his ear. A harassed-looking young woman in a brown suede coat, holding the hands of a girl of about seven and a boy of about four. An ultra-chic woman in a beige hand-knitted ensemble and boots of the same color whom I'd met casually at several cocktail parties. An elderly couple with a high-stepping black poodle on a leash, whom I recognized as friends of Guy's parents. The sort of people you might see in any small town favored by the upper middle class.

Witchcraft? In *Wessex?*

Suddenly it seemed to me that everything I had experienced could be explained away easily. Poor Sara Breed, when she told me about those hooded figures, could have been describing a scene from a movie she'd seen decades ago. As for those black candle stubs, Guy's explanation could be the right one. Prankish teenagers could have left them there. And Dilsey? Dilsey, and my beloved mother too, could have been inculcated by their mothers and grandmothers with an ancient delusion, a belief that

163

through certain rites otherwise ordinary men and women could obtain supernormal powers. The name of that delusion, in ancient times shared in one form or another by all the people on earth, was witchcraft.

And yet, and yet . . .

The way Peggy Crofton's face and Jack Payson's had seemed to alter, giving me a glimpse of something quite different behind their poised, fashionable exteriors. And the feeling I'd had in that woodland clearing yesterday, the sense of a lingering evil.

Had all of that been just my imagination? And if it had been, I wondered miserably, did that mean that Guy was right in thinking that I needed medical attention?

Suddenly I thought of my mother in our kitchen, tying up bundles of woodland plants, which practitioners of the Old Religion had used for thousands of years as remedies for all human ailments, from rheumatism to madness.

That old house, the house that had passed from my servant-girl great-grandmother to my grandmother and then to my mother. Could it be that something in the atmosphere of that house, where women of my line had lived for nearly three quarters of a century, could help me to know what to do? Perhaps the feeling that it might was just another delusion. But surely it would do no harm to go there right now, while it was still daylight. Besides, it would delay my return to that fine new house, which somehow seemed too quiet even when I had the TV or radio tuned to full volume.

I backed the Mustang into the street and then headed toward the little lake and, beyond it, the road leading past unoccupied cottages to that long-empty house. By the time I reached it, red-gold light bathed its split and curling shingles. I went up the front walk and then waded through weeds to the rear of the house.

As I'd noticed the day before, one of the two planks nailed in an X over the back door had come loose at one end from the rotting shingles. I braced my feet and pulled at the board, expecting that it would resist me, and that I would have to look around in the weeds or that caved-in shed back there for something to use as a crowbar. Instead, with a shriek of rusty nails, the other end of the plank also came free. I tossed the board into the weeds.

Although the other plank was still in place, I found I could reach the door handle. I turned it, pushed. With a complaint of long-unused hinges, the door swung back. Evidently whoever had nailed those planks against intruders had forgotten the far simpler precaution of locking the door. Either that, or the lock had rusted out.

I didn't have to remove the other diagonally nailed plank. Bending low, I ducked under it and then straightened. I was in the little back entryway with its two rust-stained laundry tubs. I walked past them into the kitchen. There was the sink board where my mother had sorted her newly gathered herbs. And there was the open doorway into what had been Sara Breed's room. I could see an iron bedstead with much of its white paint flaked away. Had it been Sara's bed? I could not be sure.

I stood motionless for a moment, listening. With the nearest living person probably miles away, the house was utterly still. And yet, curiously, I did not feel in any way discomfited by its stillness. This was not the cold silence of that other house. Instead, the atmosphere felt friendly. It was as if, in entering that rear door, I had stepped back into a time my conscious mind could not remember, a time when happiness had wrapped me like a soft blanket.

I went down the hall, past the open door of the dining room. Except for a droplight with an octagonal glass shade that looked vaguely familiar, the room appeared

165

empty. I went on down the hall and emerged into the living room.

It held only a few pieces of dust-coated furniture. A straight chair. An old black leather sofa with stuffing protruding through a burst seam. A time-spotted mirror with a tarnished gilt frame on one wall. Had this furniture been my mother's, or had it belonged to the last resident of this house, the old poet who had bought the property after my mother's death? I had no idea.

I turned and looked at the narrow box staircase leading upward. And suddenly I knew what had drawn me to this house today. I don't know how I knew. I just did.

I went up the stairs, back along a hall past open doors. One was the door to my mother's room. It held a narrow bedstead I knew had not been hers. Her bed had been a double one. It had seemed vast to me when I sometimes climbed into it in the early mornings. The next door was the bathroom's. Then I passed my old room and the spare room. Although I didn't stop to look into either of them, I caught the impression that they were empty. At the end of the hall was a closed door. I opened it. Rough plank stairs led upward. I climbed.

The attic, with its smell of dust, still retained the warmth of the long spring day. The last of the reddish sunlight came through the dust-encrusted western window into the long room with its peaked ceiling and its floor strewn with packing boxes, old trunks, and rolled-up rugs tied with twine. I walked forward several feet and then halted beneath one of the cross beams. Bending, I pulled a wooden box toward me. I stood on it and groped with my hand along the beam.

I found it almost immediately. I stepped from the box and sat down on a round-lidded trunk with the cool, smooth shape in my hand. Then I looked at it.

166

A cat, somewhat smaller than a tennis ball, lying curled up with the tip of its tail almost touching its chin. A crystal cat, looking at me from slanted eyes. A cat that seemed to grow warm on my palm as I held it.

How old was it? A hundred years? Five hundred years? More?

A memory, lost to my conscious mind until now, came back to me. My infant self, perhaps not much more than a year old, held on my mother's lap. My grandmother was in the memory too. Both women were laughing—soft, warm laughter. And I too crowed with laughter as I clasped in both small fat hands the object my grandmother had held out to me.

Had the crystal cat seemed to me just a pretty toy? Or had I sensed even then that it was a talisman, binding the three of us together, binding us also to those of our line who had gone before us? I didn't know. All I could remember was the crystal cat, and their laughing faces, and a sense of warmth and safety and happiness.

Sitting here now, with the crystal cat in my hand, I no longer felt afraid. I knew what I had to do, and I knew that I could do it.

I placed the little cat in the pocket of my old coat. Then I descended from the attic.

## TWENTY FIVE

Iᴛ ᴡᴀs almost dark by the time I reached that other house. I parked the car in the garage, went in through the back door and turned on the kitchen light.

For a moment I stood motionless in the center of the room. Then I said, into that cold silence, "All right. I'm ready for you."

I went to the living room, laid crumpled paper and some kindling and three small logs in the grate, held a match to the paper. When the fire was well caught I went back to the kitchen. From the cabinet under the sink I took out a yellow plastic bucket.

Would it be best to wear rubber gloves? Yes, I decided. I might not enjoy direct contact with what I was about to handle. I took a pair of gloves from a cabinet drawer, put them on.

Feeling a kind of grim anticipation, I thought, start with the basement.

I went down the steps to the playroom, switched on the light. On a shelf beneath the bar I found a tiny white cup filled with black liquid that had the rotten-vegetation smell of swamp water. Trying to ignore the nausea in the pit of my stomach, I lowered the cup carefully into the bucket.

Up on the first floor again, I moved with assurance from room to room. In the kitchen, behind the refrigerator, I found a small, stoppered bottle containing a dead mouse. Still battling nausea, I placed it in the bucket beside the tiny cup.

From the under surface of the phone table in the hall, I ripped loose a bundle of dark red feathers, which had been held in place by a strip of gummed tape. Chicken feathers? They looked like it. And I had read somewhere that the feathers of domestic fowl were used by practitioners of black magic. Fleetingly I thought of the elegant Peggy Crofton tying up this bundle of feathers with a length of black thread, just like some obeah woman in a Caribbean slum.

In the dining room I found, atop the tall china closet, a thick white saucer holding some gray pastelike substance. I placed it in the bucket and then went into the living room. Far back in the liquor cabinet I found another stoppered bottle. This one contained a long-dead frog. Its dry skin rattled against the glass as I lowered it into the bucket.

Upstairs, in the bedroom Guy and I had occupied, I turned back one corner of the rug. Another small bundle of feathers, this time of white and black as well as dark red. I put them in the bucket.

Out in the hall I paused for a moment. Were there any more of them up here? I somehow felt sure there were not.

I descended to the living room. The logs were blazing now. I put the fire screen aside, quickly tossed the contents of the bucket onto the fire, replaced the screen.

Standing there, I watched and listened as the fire dealt with what I'd fed it. A sizzling sound. That must be the black liquid and gray paste. The tinkle of the bottles bursting. A blend of odors that tied my stomach into an even tighter knot.

But still I stood there, for twenty minutes or maybe even half an hour, while the logs and what I'd thrown on them burned. Finally I went out in the lower hall and listened. Except for the popping noise made by embers of the dying fire, the house was silent. But now it was an ordinary silence, a mere absence of sound.

I went back to the fireplace and set the screen aside. With the poker I stirred the embers to speed their extinction. I saw bits of glass and crockery among the fire's remains. The sight of them did not bother me. They were harmless now, just something to be dumped in the trash. In the morning, when the fireplace was completely cold, I would take the bottle and dish fragments out.

I hung the poker in its stand, put the fire screen in place, turned out the lights. Out in the kitchen, I rinsed the plastic bucket with hot water from the tap and peeled off the rubber gloves. I felt vast relief, and even triumph, but I felt tired too, bone tired. All the accumulated fatigue of the last two crowded days had caught up with me.

I felt too tired to even think of food. And upstairs I felt almost too tired to undress. But I took off my old coat, then the rest of my clothes, slipped a nightgown over my head and fell into bed. Almost instantly, I slept.

Smell of smoke.

I sat bolt upright in the darkness. Somewhere in the house, something was burning.

I threw back the covers, hurried out into the hall, flipped on the light. No visible smoke, but out here the smell of something burning was stronger than it had been in the bedroom. Swiftly I went down the stairs, reached inside the living-room doorway, switched on the overhead light.

Near the fireplace a thick spiral of smoke, shot with pale flames, rose from the seat of a Queen Anne chair upholstered with crewel embroidery.

I made a quick decision. I could handle it. No need to flee the house. But if I'd remained asleep even a few minutes longer—

I dashed to the coffee table, snatched up a silver pitcher holding the daffodils I'd brought into the house several days before in hopes of making the place seem a little friendlier. Upending the pitcher, I doused the chair seat with both water and flowers. The flickers of flame vanished. Steam billowed upward.

The chair still might be burning, deeper in the upholstery. I ran to the kitchen, took down the small fire extinguisher affixed to the wall near the refrigerator. As I ran back toward the living room, I asked myself how the chair could have caught fire. Had I, in replacing the fire screen, left a gap through which an ember had popped out? In my bone-weariness, I might have.

Back in the living room, I turned the fire extinguisher upside down, pressed the button, sprayed the chair with a smothering white foam. It wasn't until I was sure that the fire was completely out that I set down the extinguisher and turned my attention to the fire screen.

Yes, there was a gap an inch or so wide between one end of the screen and the fireplace facing.

*Had* I left it like that? Or was it that those objects I had thrown on the fire had not been entirely destroyed after all? Had at least one of them retained enough vicious power—

No! I was sure all of them had been consumed, except

171

for a few bits of glass and crockery. I shoved the screen back into place and then looked down through the mesh at the few tiny embers still glowing among the gray ash.

Suddenly I felt my body turning cold. There was still a third explanation. Had someone invaded this house and set a fire in that chair? An upholstery fire, one of the most dangerous kinds, which, soon spreading, would have sent billows of smothering smoke up to my bedroom. A fire that the insurance people would have attributed to an improperly placed fire screen.

Was someone in the house right now?

I thought, I must get out of here.

But even as I whirled around to run from the room, reason reasserted itself. If there had been someone in this house while I was putting out the fire, someone bent upon harming me, he or she would have tried to do so by now.

Nevertheless, I didn't want to spend the rest of the night here. I went swiftly up the stairs. And once I was inside the bedroom I turned the door's thumb latch. From downstairs came the sound of the tall clock in the hall, striking twelve-thirty.

Hurriedly I dressed, checked my handbag to be sure I had my car keys. I opened the closet door and thrust my hand into the pocket of my old raincoat. Yes, the little cat was still there, smooth and cool to my fingers. I started to take the coat off its hanger.

Footsteps, coming along the lower hall.

Through the pounding of my heart I heard them reach the foot of the stairs, start climbing. They reached the upper hall, moved to the bedroom door, stopped.

Frozen, I watched the doorknob turn.

"Linda? Are you in there, Linda?"

Feeling faint with relief, I went to the door, turned the

172

thumb latch. Guy came into the room. Whimpering, I flung myself against him.

Although his arm tightened around me, he didn't ask what was the matter. Instead he said, "There's smoke downstairs."

"There was a fire. In one of the living-room chairs."

"You're sure it's out?"

"Yes."

"Then let's go."

"Go? Where?" I leaned back in the circle of his arms. For the first time I noticed how white and strained his face was.

"I'm taking you to New York. I'll leave you there with the Cartwrights."

"Leave me! But—"

"I'll have things to attend to here. Or rather, people to attend to."

"Guy—"

"Nicole came to the motel to see me tonight. She was in a hysterical rage. She'd found out who her Frenchman was going to marry. It's her Aunt Peggy."

"Peggy! Peggy Crofton?"

"Sure. Nicole is young and beautiful, but Peggy's the one with the money. Nicole came back early from a shopping trip to Hartford this afternoon and caught Jean-Paul and Peggy in bed."

"And they told her—"

"They didn't have a chance to tell her anything then. She bolted from the house and drove away. But later she decided to call Peggy. Jean-Paul answered the phone and told her she might as well know the truth. He and Peggy were going to get married. Now where is your suitcase? On the closet shelf, isn't it?"

Bewildered, I watched him take my suitcase down

from the shelf, open it on the bed. "Guy, you haven't told me why you want me to go to New—"

"Nicole spilled everything to me."

"Everything?"

"About the—the rottenness Peggy Crofton brought to this town about twenty-five years ago. But start packing, Linda. I want to get you out of here."

We both packed, moving back and forth between the bureau and the suitcase on the bed. And while we packed, Guy talked. "You were right about those meetings in the woods. They're all women, except for Jack Payson."

He reached into an opened drawer, took out several pairs of pantyhose still in their plastic envelopes and laid them in the suitcase. "Maybe their mumbo jumbo is just that—mumbo jumbo. Maybe they don't really have any special powers. But God knows the *intent* behind the things they do is evil. Nicole told me of the things Peggy brags about. Blinding a teenage boy, for instance, some kid who'd destroyed something or other on her property. Maybe the kid would have lost his sight anyway. But the point is that she *thinks* she blinded him. And then—"

He broke off so abruptly that I was sure he had been about to speak of what happened to my mother. Instead he said, after a moment, "Peggy had Jack Payson put some things in this house before we came back here to live in it. Spells, I suppose you could call them. Anyway, sickening stuff, like a dried-up frog and bundles of feathers."

"I know. I found them and destroyed them."

"Found them? How? No, you can tell me later. You think we've packed enough stuff?"

I nodded.

"Then where's your coat?" He jerked my rain-or-shine coat from its hanger. "Will this one do?"

"Yes."

As he helped me into it I asked, "Is Nicole still here? If Peggy and Jack find out she told you—"

"Probably she's many miles from here by now. She told me she intended to start back to San Francisco right tonight. Now come on. Let's go."

## TWENTY-SIX

WE STEPPED out the front door into the light of a moon a little way past its full. The car Guy had rented stood in the drive. "We'll take this one. I like the way it handles," he said and put my suitcase in the trunk.

We got into the convertible's front seat. He backed out of the drive and turned toward the road that paralleled the river. I asked tautly, "Guy, why are you coming back here after you leave me with the Cartwrights?"

"I have to, for at least a little while."

"But why?" I cried. "Why can't we both stay in New York?"

"We can. And we will, if you want to. But first I'm going to deal with those two."

"Deal?"

"Drive them out of town. Only a few people know what they've been doing. The vast majority of people in town would be outraged if they knew. When I brought you to Wessex, I told you that Peggy Crofton ran the town. Well, she's not going to much longer."

Fear squeezed my heart. To hold on to her power in the town, Peggy would use any weapon she could. "Please, darling. Don't try to oppose her." I thought of what had happened to my mother. And now perhaps Guy . . .

He turned onto the river road. "I have to, Linda. Now that I know, I have to do something about it. Even if what they call witchcraft is only self-delusion, the town must be rid of them. And if it *isn't* delusion—"

He broke off and then said, after a moment, "Nicole told me the names of the women Peggy has managed to involve in her—rottenness. I know most of them fairly well. Some are like Nicole herself, on the feather-brained side. All of them have time on their hands. It's not hard to see how bored, idle women might . . . But once Peggy Crofton and Jack Payson are out of the picture, those women will go back to their bridge games, or crewel embroidery, or whatever."

He paused, and then asked, "You said that an armchair caught fire?"

"Yes, that Queen Anne wing chair."

"How did it start?"

"I don't know. For a while I thought it might be . . . But now I think I just didn't place the screen properly. I guess I'll never know for sure."

He didn't answer.

We turned onto Main Street. The shops and the apartments above them were dark. Except for the blue light in front of the police station and the amber glow of the handsome streetlights made to resemble nineteenth-century gas lamps, there was no illumination at all. At this hour, Main Street was completely deserted.

No, not quite deserted. Feeling the hair prickle on the back of my neck, I became aware of the sound of a following car.

I turned and looked through the rear window. It was back there about three hundred yards. In the bright moonlight its shape was visible, despite the dazzle of its headlights.

177

I looked at Guy's set profile. "There's a car—"

"I know. It turned off the river road onto Main Street about a minute ago."

"Jack Payson's car?"

"Has to be. It's a Bentley. I can tell by the set of its headlights. The only other Bentley in town is owned by the Pawleys, and they're in Europe." He paused. "Payson has a passenger."

Peggy.

I'd seen no cars parked along our street when we left the house. But they must have been there, parked in some driveway, waiting to see what we would do.

I said sickly, "They must have guessed—"

"That Nicole might have come to me and spilled her guts? Yes."

"Guy, do you have a gun in this car?" He shook his head. "Do you think that they have one?"

He said, after a moment, "Probably they do. But they won't use it here in town. Not unless we turn around and start back toward the police station. They might very well use it then."

I plunged my hand into my coat pocket and grasped the little crystal cat. After a moment it seemed to throb against my finger. It could counter at least some of the special powers of someone like Peggy. It had done so tonight. But could it protect us against an ordinary weapon like a gun?

It had not protected my mother against the barbiturate that weak-witted Sara Breed had placed in her food.

"Guy, what are we—"

"We're going to try to get to the interstate as fast as we can. Now listen to me, Linda. Right now they're hanging back. That must mean they hope we don't realize who they are. But once we're out of town—"

"They'll try to catch us!"

"But they won't. Bentleys aren't built for speed."

"This is a rental car. You can't know how much it has been misused. If you try to get speed out of it, you may find—"

I broke off. From the way Guy's lips tightened, I knew he wished we'd taken the Mustang. But all he said was, "Just the same, we'll outrun them. And once we're on the interstate, there'll be plenty of traffic, even this time of night. It will be easy to lose them entirely."

We were in the residential part of Main Street now. The fine old houses sat dark and silent behind their deep lawns. The streetlights, more widely spaced here, cast circles of light on the deserted sidewalks.

We passed the last houses. No sidewalks now and no streetlights, just the little lake sparkling in the moonlight. Beyond it the woodland began.

As soon as we'd entered the wood, following the moonlit road now spotted with the moving shadows of tree branches, Guy stepped hard on the throttle. The car shot forward.

I looked back. Plainly he had caught them by surprise. The distance between us had lengthened. My heart bounded with hope. Then, only seconds later, I became aware that the Bentley's headlights seemed to have grown in size.

"Guy! they're—"

"I know. Get down." Then, as I sat paralyzed: "Get *down,* damn it! And stay down, no matter what happens."

I curled up on the seat then, lying on my side. But even though I could not see the Bentley, I knew it was gaining. I could tell by the way the headlights' glow bathing our car's interior seemed to grow brighter.

179

Guy spun the wheel. With a slithering of tires, we turned right. Mouth dry with fear, I knew what that meant. He'd given up hope of outrunning them to the interstate.

But his abrupt turn off the state road had brought us at least temporary advantage. The glow of the Bentley's headlights no longer filled the car. Then, seconds later, it was there again, brightening inexorably.

Guy made another sharp turn, to the left this time. Again the Bentley fell back and then, after a few moments, began to catch up. Guy made another skidding turn, again to the left.

Memory stirred. We'd followed this route once before, my first Saturday in Wessex, the day of our picnic. Suddenly I felt almost sure I knew what Guy was planning.

Would it work? Probably, if neither of them knew about the danger of that winding, rutted road. And they might not know. Neither of them were natives of this area. And it was hard to imagine either of them as deer hunters or picnickers.

But if they did know, then we would be the ones trapped. Trapped between the Bentley and a stretch of road so narrowed by erosion that it would be deadly even in the daytime.

Perhaps two minutes passed, although to me, curled up on the leather seat, it seemed many times that. In the steadily brightening glow of the Bentley's headlights, I could see Guy's foot pressing the throttle to the floorboards.

A shatter of glass, a whining sound above my curled body. I turned my head and looked up. The whole right side of the windshield was opaque now, its shattered glass surrounding a bullet hole. Although I did not sit up to look, I knew there must be a similar hole in the convertible's rear window.

Guy warned, "Keep down!"

Another bullet. This one did not come through the rear window, but it did hit the car. I heard the spanging sound of the steel bullet against the convertible's steel body.

Guy jerked the wheel. With a lurch that almost threw me against the dashboard, the car started down a steep incline. I was sure where we were now. I heard the squeal of the Bentley's brakes.

I raised my head just high enough to see over the seat back. Plainly Guy's sharp turn onto the track leading down to the river had caught Jack Payson by surprise. Up there on the road, the Bentley was backing up. Quickly, before Guy had to tell me to, I lowered my head.

The convertible rattled over the bridge's planks. Then, in second gear, we began to climb. Before we reached the road's first curve, the glow of the Bentley's headlights was filling the car. But evidently unfamiliarity with the road, and perhaps that warning sign back there, had slowed them considerably. The light of their headlamps vanished when we went around the curve, not to reappear until after we had rounded two more curves, and even then it was fainter than before.

"Now listen carefully," Guy said. "Remember our picnic?"

"Yes." To my own ears my voice sounded high and thin.

"Just around the next curve is the turnout where we parked that day. When we reach it, I'm going to stop just long enough for you to get out. Climb the hillside and hide among the trees. And stay there until I come back for you."

I loathed those two people in the Bentley more than I'd realized I could loathe any human beings. Peggy Crofton had killed my mother, just as surely as if she had

181

done it with her own hands. And now she and her cousin were determined to kill the two of us. And yet, even though I knew something of the sort had to be done, I felt sick at the thought of the trap Guy was laying for them.

"Do you understand me, Linda?"

"Yes."

He rounded a curve, stopped. "Quickly!"

I got out of the car. He closed the door softly, drove on. I climbed the overgrown path leading up from beside the cut in the hillside, my feet sliding on the grass. Then I crouched beside a tree. I could see the road, but I was sure that those two, intent on their quarry, would not look up and see me.

The sound of Guy's car had ceased. In my mind's eye I could see him sitting behind the wheel of the motionless convertible, just around the next curve. No, no! Not behind the wheel. Surely he realized that if the Bentley slammed into his car, both vehicles might go hurtling down the hillside. Surely now he was standing up above the road, waiting.

Sound of the Bentley's engine, growing louder. I saw the loom of its headlights even before it came around the curve. As it passed, I caught a glimpse of Peggy in the passenger seat, her face looking like carved white stone in the dashboard's upward-striking light.

I waited. Surely Guy was standing in some safe place. Surely he was. The sound of the Bentley's engine altered slightly as it rounded the curve up ahead.

A woman's scream, despairing and enraged. Then another sound, high-pitched, prolonged—the shriek of metal surfaces against each other and against rocks and trees and bushes. Almost as clearly as if it were happening before my eyes, I visualized the Bentley rolling over and over down the hillside.

Utter silence for perhaps three seconds. Then the sound of an explosion. Even on this side of the curve I could see, mingling with the moonlight, the refracted, wavering glow of the burning car.

Or was there more than one car down there?

Bathed in sweat, forgetting entirely my promise to Guy, I stood up and descended, on legs that felt weak, to the road. I was hurrying toward the curve when I saw Guy coming around it.

We went into each other's arms. After a while I said, "Are they—"

"They must be. I didn't see either of them fall out of the car. But I'll go down there and make sure."

I shuddered. "Did they hit your car?"

"No. He must have jerked the wheel to the left instinctively when he saw my car standing there, right in front of him."

"What shall we—"

"There are highway patrol phones on the interstate. Without giving my name, I'll call and say a crashed car has caught fire, and tell them where they can find it. What I may tell the police later I just don't know. Right now all I know is that I want to get you safely to the Cartwrights. Now wait just a few minutes more."

He walked back around the curve. I waited, sickly aware of that reddish glow and trying not to think of those two evil, handsome people down there in the burning car. Then at last I saw the convertible's taillights as he backed it around the curve. In the turnout space, he maneuvered the car until it was headed down the road. Then he swung the door back for me to get in.

As we descended the rutted road, I didn't ask if they were dead. I knew that if either of them had been alive, he would have said so.

We started across the bridge. I asked, "Will you stop at the other end?"

"What is it?"

"I'll tell you afterward. Please just let me out and then wait for me for a minute or two."

At the far end of the bridge he stopped the car. I walked back over the planks to about the middle of the bridge. Standing at the iron rail, I looked down at the swift river, touched here and there by foam that appeared blue-white in the moonlight. At last I reached into my coat pocket and brought out the little crystal cat.

It lay on my palm, giving back the moonlight. Again I wondered how many centuries old it was, and where it had originated. In Tuscany, among the Etruscan worshipers of the Earth Mother? Perhaps. Or perhaps in Britain, at the time the Druids were building Stonehenge. Whatever its age and origin, it was a talisman of powers that set the Old Believer apart from ordinary people.

But I wanted no supernormal powers. What I wanted, and all I wanted, was to live out my life as an ordinary woman, with an ordinary woman's chances of happiness.

And yet, as I looked down at this little object on my palm, I felt a wrenching sense of loss at the thought of renouncing this link with my gentle mother, and with my mother's mother, and with all those others of my line, stretching back and back.

It cost me an effort to hold my hand out over the rail, palm up. Nevertheless, I did it.

I made myself turn my hand over. "Good-bye, little cat," I said aloud.

Glittering in the moonlight, it fell down and down to the foaming river.

I turned and walked back to where Guy waited.